# SECRETS OF THE SNOW GLOBE

## MENACING MAGIC

## Anne Wan

## Illustrated by Dawn Larder

# Contents

For
Julie, Tim
*and*
Barbara

# Chapter 1
## Jack's Secret

'Jack, where are you?' Louisa pushed open the shed door. Inside, her brother, Jack, was kneeling on the floor beside a rack of shelves lined with paint pots. He jumped guiltily and shoved something behind a tin on the bottom shelf.

'What do you want?' he snapped.

Louisa flinched. Jack hadn't been the same since they had returned from their adventure inside the snow globe six months ago. She was getting used to his secretive behaviour and his short temper – but she didn't like it. 'Grandma sent me. Lunch is ready.'

'I'll be there in a minute,' said Jack.

Louisa's eyes darted to the tin on the bottom shelf. Jack edged sideways, blocking her view. 'I said I'm coming.'

'What have you hidden behind there?' She stepped towards him.

Jack glared at her. 'None of your business! Push off!'

His words stung. 'There's no need to be rude,' she said. 'I'm fed up of you hiding things from me and snapping at me.'

'Well, I'm fed up of your snooping. Leave me alone!' He jumped to his feet, knocking into Grandad's bike. He grabbed the handlebars just in time to stop it crashing onto the lawn mower. Louisa seized the opportunity. She leapt at the paint pot and yanked it off the shelf. Lying behind it in the dust was a dirty diamond snowflake!

'What do you think you're doing?' said Jack, snatching up the diamond, his eyes blazing.

'Me? What are *you* doing with that snowflake?' said Louisa. 'It's from the snow globe, isn't it? You stole it!'

The fire in Jack's eyes fizzled out. He hung his head.

'Is this what you've been hiding from me?'

He nodded miserably.

'I don't believe it!' scolded Louisa. 'After all the trouble Harry caused when he stole the diamond snowflakes from his brother, now you've done the same thing! What were you thinking?'

Jack held the snowflake protectively to his chest. 'It's George's snowflake – the one we used on our quest to reach the Miser's castle. It helped us when we were in trouble, like George promised.'

'How did you…?'

'Before we left the music festival I saw George's coat lying over a chair. Everyone was busy celebrating. I slipped it from his pocket. I was curious to see if its magic would work in our world,' said Jack.

'You thought it would help you?'

'I hoped it would. I wore the snowflake during the school play,' Jack explained. 'I was worried about forgetting my lines. I thought it would help me to remember them.'

'But you forgot your lines! You started singing the national anthem in the middle of Act Two! The audience didn't know whether to stand or ignore it as some kind of joke!' said Louisa.

'I know. The kids at school still hum the tune and snigger when they see me.'

'That's awful,' said Louisa. 'I wonder why the diamond snowflake didn't help you?'

Jack shrugged. 'I don't know. I thought it would help me remember the steps in that awful maypole dance too. Instead, halfway through the dance I had this overwhelming urge to spin around on the spot. I couldn't help it.'

'I remember! You looked like a ballerina doing a pirouette!'

'Don't remind me,' Jack groaned. 'Mr Wilson still hasn't forgiven me.'

'I'm not surprised. There was chaos! When the maypole crashed down, it almost landed on his head!'

'That snowflake has wrecked my chances in

rugby too. I wore it when I played in matches, hoping it would help me to score extra tries. But it didn't help at all. Every time I had the ball, I dropped it or kicked it off the pitch!'

'So that's why the coach moved you from team captain to reserve player,' said Louisa.

'He had no choice. My rubbish playing cost the team the final three matches of the season.'

'No wonder your team-mates don't speak to you any more. I'm not surprised you're miserable, Jack.'

'This stupid snowflake has ruined everything!' He held the diamond snowflake up to the light. The gem that had once glistened radiantly in the snow globe was now dirty, grey and dull.

'It's filthy!' said Louisa. 'It needs cleaning.'

'That's what I was trying to do before you burst in on me. It's been turning grey for a while. I found Grandad's silver polish on the shelf. Thought it might work. I've tried everything – soap, water, that spray stuff Grandma uses to clean the bathroom. Whatever I try, the diamond stays that yucky colour.'

Louisa took the snowflake and turned it

over in her hand. 'Maybe it's going bad because you took it out of the snow globe. Grandma said that she and her father found the diamond snowflakes inside the mountain in the globe. That's where they belong.'

'You mean the snowflake's magic only works properly inside the globe?' said Jack.

'Maybe. In our world its magic is…reversed. Instead of making life better, it makes it worse.'

'I knew I shouldn't have stolen it,' Jack mumbled. 'I wish I could give it back. I hoped the snow globe would transport me to I-Sing again.'

'So you could return the snowflake to George?' Louisa asked.

'Yes. I've even packed a bag ready. It's hidden in the lounge, behind the sofa. Silly of me.'

'It's not silly. It's horrible when you have to own up to doing something wrong. At least you want to put it right. We have to return the snowflake to the snow globe.'

'*We?* Well, I suppose that now you know about the snowflake, you might as well come too,' said Jack.

'Try stopping me! I'll see George and Harry again. Maybe Daisy too,' said Louisa. 'It wasn't a silly idea to pack a bag, Jack, it was genius! We've got to be ready to shrink back inside the snow globe!'

## Chapter 2
## Earthquake

Two weeks passed before Louisa and Jack visited Grandma's house again for a sleepover. Louisa had made a list of items she would need inside the snow globe. 'I've packed warm boots and thick socks. My feet were freezing last time!' she told Jack, checking her rucksack.

'I couldn't fit my boots in my bag. I've packed extra chocolate, though,' Jack replied, tucking his rucksack and boots behind Grandma's sofa.

'And the snowflake?'

'In my wallet. The one Grandad gave me.'

'Right, you two,' said Grandma, appearing in the doorway dressed in her gardening clothes. 'I'm replanting the flower pots this morning. Either of you want to help?'

Jack shuddered at the mention of gardening. 'Thanks, but we'd like to play indoors,' he said.

'Well, join me if you change your mind.'

Louisa heard the back door close. 'I like planting. It's a shame I can't help Grandma.'

'Gardening is too much like hard work!' said Jack. 'Besides, we have to stay in the lounge in case the snow globe lights up and the magic begins to work.'

Louisa peered into the display cabinet at the snow globe. Inside the globe, the picturesque village of I-Sing nestled peacefully on the slopes of the miniature mountain. 'I wish we could force the magic to work, then we could shrink inside the snow globe straight away. It could be a long wait.'

'I wish I hadn't left my DS at home,' complained Jack. 'I'm going to be bored stiff.'

'Monopoly?' said Louisa, sliding the board game out from beneath the coffee table.

Jack scowled. 'You know I hate that game.'

'Only because I always beat you!' Louisa grinned. She set out the pieces and counted the money with slick precision.

'Well, since there's nothing better to do.' Jack slumped onto the floor and began to play.

After several hours, Grandad poked his head around the door. 'You've been here all morning! Do you want to come for a walk with me and the dogs?'

'Er, no thanks. We're in the middle of Monopoly,' said Louisa triumphantly as Jack handed her £2,000 for landing on Mayfair.

'Suit yourselves.' Grandad pulled on his tweed flat cap. He whistled for the dogs and left.

'How much longer have we got to play this tedious game?' groaned Jack.

'As long as it takes for the snow globe to—' Before Louisa could finish her sentence, a brilliant light shone across the room. 'The snow globe! Jack, it's working! Quick!'

Louisa snatched her coat from the chair and dived for the rucksacks hidden behind the sofa. 'Here!' she said, tossing Jack his boots and bag.

Jack caught them. He rattled the door of the cabinet in which the snow globe was displayed, shining brightly.

'It won't open! It's locked!'

'What? It wasn't locked before!'

'Where does Grandma keep the key?'

'I don't know! Try the top of the cabinet.'

Jack balanced on the arm of the chair and

fumbled along the top of the cabinet. 'It's not here! Check the mantelpiece. Sometimes Grandma puts things behind the clock for safekeeping.'

Louisa rummaged behind the clock.

'Hurry, Louisa! We need to get the snow globe out now! It's rising off the shelf!'

'Got it!' she cried as her fingers closed around the smooth key. She threw it at Jack.

He unlocked the cabinet door and flung it open. The snow globe flew into the centre of the room. With a loud *CRACK* the glass dome ripped apart from the base. Above them, snow cascaded from the dome.

'I don't like this bit!' cried Louisa as they were propelled into the air in the middle of a spiralling blizzard.

'Me neither!' yelled Jack, turning slightly green. 'It's too much flying!'

The whirlwind stopped. Louisa and Jack dangled high above the floor like puppets. The sensation of being hugged by a giant bear crept over Louisa.

'We're shrinking!' cried Jack.

Louisa felt as though she would shrink away to nothing – then they began to fall. 'Argh!' she yelled, plunging headfirst towards the snow globe base. She had braced herself for the moment of impact when they slowed, almost to a halt, then dropped gently in a thick bank of snow. Louisa gasped as the icy air caught in her throat. She could hear Jack flailing beside her. She scrambled to her feet. A row of wooden chalets ran alongside them, dripping with icicles.

'I-Sing!' she breathed. She gazed at the jagged mountain peak that rose beyond the rooftops. 'Jack, we've done it! We're in the village inside the snow globe!'

Filling the square was a crowd of villagers, their backs to Jack and Louisa. They were absorbed by something on the far side and seemed unaware of their sudden arrival.

'What's everyone staring at?' said Jack.

'I can't see.' Louisa stood on tiptoe to gain

a better view when suddenly the ground began to tremble.

Jack stumbled. 'What's going on?' he cried, growing pale with fear.

Shouts of panic rang from the crowd. The mountainside groaned. The ground juddered. Louisa swayed as if trying to balance on a rope bridge.

'Earthquake!' cried the villagers. 'It's happening again! Earthquake!'

Louisa's blood fizzed. 'Since when did I-Sing have earthquakes?'

'Dunno!' cried Jack, dodging a tile that had slipped from the roof above them.

The earth rumbled like thunder. Anxious voices called out, 'The sculptures!'

'Quick! Harry, help!'

Louisa noticed the stooped figure of their friend, Harry, standing on the steps of the Great

Hall. Across the square, mothers were frantically gathering their children. Friends were holding on to each other for support. Amid the chaos, Louisa glimpsed a row of stunning ice sculptures displayed on a long table. They teetered – then toppled towards the ground.

Suddenly, the earth stopped trembling. The mountain was silent. Louisa watched in amazement as the carved ice statues paused in mid-air. Harry's gloved hands stretched out towards the sculptures. He seemed to have halted their fall by some invisible power. He raised his arms. The sculptures lifted into the air then returned gently to their display stands. Not one of them was damaged.

'Bravo, Harry!'

'Hurray!' The crowd cheered and clapped.

Recovering her breath, Louisa shivered in the icy breeze.

'Put your coat on!' said Jack, taking his coat from his rucksack and pulling on his boots.

Louisa looked down at her hands. She was still clutching her coat. As she put it on, she heard a warm, melodious voice above the cheers: 'Thank you, Harry, for your assistance!'

A hush fell over the crowd. They turned towards the speaker. Louisa followed their gaze. At the end of the row of ice sculptures, on a high platform, stood a beautiful lady. Dressed in a green velvet robe, she looked regal and calm. Although she seemed to be shorter than the women of I-Sing, she stood upright, her shoulders back, her chin raised, giving off an air of serenity and confidence. A feeling of reassurance settled like a snug blanket around Louisa's shoulders.

'Once again we, the people of I-Sing, are grateful to you, Harry, for your timely assistance.

What would we do without you?' A forced smile spread across her tight lips.

The crowd clapped their approval.

'Who is she trying to fool?' Jack whispered in Louisa's ear. 'She looks furious, having to say thank you to Harry.'

'Rubbish!' Louisa retorted. 'I think she's wonderful!'

'Who is she?' said Jack. 'The crowd seem to love her.'

A child poked her head around the skirts of a lady in front of them. She took her thumb out of her mouth. 'That's the Velvet Lady!' she said, wide-eyed, then turned away.

'The Velvet Lady!' Louisa repeated. 'Her name certainly fits.'

'I commend you all for your bravery as we withstand yet another earthquake here in I-Sing. I assure you that I, as Mayoress, will stop at nothing to find a solution to this problem. However, now that the earthquake is over, I can announce the winner of I-Sing's first ever Ice Sculpture competition. First prize goes to Madame Étoile for your stunning kestrel in flight!'

## Chapter 3
## Good as New

'Madame Étoile?' gasped Louisa. 'Jack, wasn't Madame the old lady who gave Grandma the riddle when she arrived in I-Sing as a girl? She must be ancient by now!'

Jack nodded. 'Grandma said that Madame was obsessed with birds. This woman has carved a kestrel. It could be her!'

They watched as a an elderly lady stepped towards the platform to receive her prize, clutching a thick shawl around her shoulders. A ginger-haired guard dressed in a green uniform reached out to assist her. 'I don't need help, young man!' the old woman snapped, snatching away her hand. 'I can manage perfectly well.'

'She's certainly feisty, just like Grandma's description of Madame. It must be the same person,' whispered Jack.

The Velvet Lady presented Madame with an oval glass plaque. 'Congratulations. A superb effort.'

Madame gave a curt nod. She turned and waved to the crowd, who applauded her affectionately.

'Well done to everyone who entered the competition,' continued the Velvet Lady. 'With so many wonderful entries, I think you'll agree it has been a tremendous success. To complete this celebration, everyone is welcome at the Great Hall where Harry has provided refreshments.' She smiled at the crowd then left the platform, escorted by a second guard. The crowd broke into excited chatter and dispersed.

'Let's go to the hall and find Harry,' said Louisa. 'George is sure to be with him.'

Jack agreed. They picked up their rucksacks from the snow and joined the bustling crowd heading for the Great Hall. Before they could reach the steps, a weedy, middle-aged man in a colourful patchwork coat stepped into their path. Louisa drew back from the bizarre-looking figure. With a bulging rucksack on his back and a pouch that jingled with coins strapped around his waist, he looked like a one-man music band and a market seller rolled into one.

'Can I interest you youngsters in a new scarf?' he chirped. 'Made of llama wool and guaranteed to keep out the cold!' He gave them

a crafty smile and opened the left side of his long coat to reveal a display of scarves. His pale brown eyes darted to Louisa. 'Maybe a doll for the lady?' He tugged a string on his rucksack. A flap opened, revealing a display of small porcelain-faced dolls.

'Wow!' breathed Louisa, moving closer.

'We don't want anything, thank you,' said Jack, pulling Louisa's sleeve.

The pedlar tipped his worn bowler hat. 'As you wish.' He turned to a nearby gentleman. 'Silk handkerchief, sir? Finest quality!'

'He's a shifty one,' Jack whispered.

'I suppose so. I liked the dolls, though,' replied Louisa. 'I wish you hadn't pulled me away.'

'I don't trust him. Dodgy goods. I bet the dolls would fall apart in a day. Come on. Let's find Harry.'

The Great Hall buzzed with lively conversation punctuated with bursts of laughter. The villagers sat at long tables piled high with iced gingerbread biscuits and fruit buns. At the table closest to the door, Harry was delighting a group of children by making a pyramid of chocolates appear from nowhere. As Jack and Louisa approached, a great white cat rose to his feet beside Harry and glared at them.

'It's Ice-Claw!' said Jack warily, recognising Harry's pet snow leopard. 'Last time we saw him, he almost ate us!'

'He must be safe, otherwise Harry wouldn't bring him out with so many people,' said Louisa. 'Look! George is here too!' She pointed to an elderly gentleman sitting on the opposite side of the table. 'George!' she cried, pushing through the crowd to meet him.

'Louisa? Jack?' George's wrinkled face rippled into a broad smile, and he stood to greet them. 'This is a lovely surprise!' He gave Louisa a big hug and shook Jack's hand. 'My, how you've grown, Louisa. You're almost as tall as Jack!'

Jack grimaced. Louisa grinned and drew herself up even taller.

'Well, I never!' cried Harry, beaming. 'How wonderful to see you!' He turned to the group of children that surrounded him. 'Right, off you go! That's enough chocolate for now.'

They moaned, disappointed, then ran off to fill their plates with gingerbread.

'It's such a surprise to see you both,' said George. 'We hoped you'd find your way back to I-Sing one day, but we weren't sure if it was possible.'

'We weren't sure either!' said Jack.

'I love your new cloak, Harry,' said Louisa. 'It's a lovely blue.'

'Really?' Harry tugged the collar self-consciously.

'I told him he couldn't wear those sinister black cloaks any more,' said George. 'Not now that the villagers are friendly with him.'

'Blue suits you,' said Louisa.

'Thank you,' replied Harry, giving a little bow. 'Please, you must sit down.' He motioned to two chairs.

Louisa was grateful to have somewhere to rest so she could change her soggy trainers for the thick socks and warm boots she had packed.

'You came prepared, I see.' George chuckled. 'I'm so glad to see you again. It must be months since you were last here.'

'More than six,' said Louisa, pulling on her boots.

Jack hung back, staring at Ice-Claw.

'He won't harm you,' said Harry. 'How about some hot chocolate?'

'Yes, please!' they chorused.

Harry clapped his gloved hands. Two mugs of hot chocolate appeared on the table. Louisa sipped the steaming liquid. 'Ahhh,' she sighed.

'Good?' said Harry.

'The best!' Louisa answered, feeling the chocolatey sweetness tingle through her body. 'Food always tastes better in I-Sing!'

Gingerly, Jack sat on a chair, keeping a watchful eye on Ice-Claw.

'So tell us what you have been up to since we last saw you,' said George, his grey eyes shining behind his oval spectacles.

Jack turned pale and stared at his mug. Louisa spoke. 'Nothing much. But when we left I-Sing and returned to Grandma's house, we discovered that she knew about the snow globe's magic too. She told us her story.'

Harry and George listened, fascinated, as Louisa recounted Grandma's adventure in the snow globe as a girl – how she had searched for her father and been led into the mountain using a riddle given to her by Madame Étoile.

George's tufty eyebrows shot up at the mention of Madame Étoile. 'Your grandma met Madame?'

'Yes. She said that Madame was an woman old then!' Louisa replied.

'We've known Madame since we were boys,' said Harry. 'Last month the village celebrated her hundred and twentieth birthday. She still doesn't show signs of ageing or slowing down. She's got more energy than I have!'

George chuckled. Louisa continued her story, explaining how Grandma found the magical diamond snowflakes deep inside the heart of the mountain.

'Our snowflakes came from inside the mountain?' said Harry.

'Mr Kraus tried to steal them. Grandma and Kraus battled for them in the clearing in the forest, and they were lost,' explained Louisa.

'Mr Kraus? Our old teacher?' said Harry. 'I never liked him.'

'So the diamonds fell in the clearing?' said George. 'Well, that explains how they got there. That's where we found them when we were boys! Do you remember, Harry? When we built the snowman?'

'I remember.' Harry nodded solemnly and stared at the table.

Louisa recalled how he had told them he'd stolen the snowflakes from George when they were boys. Even now the memory seemed to cause him pain.

'Tell us what has been happening here,' said Louisa, changing the subject. 'That earthquake was terrifying!'

'The earthquakes started not long after you left. At first, they were very mild. So small, it was easy to miss them,' said George.

'But gradually they became stronger and more frequent,' said Harry. 'Now they're almost daily.'

'If we didn't have Harry here to stop them and mend people's property, I-Sing would be in ruins,' finished George. 'It's almost as if the mountain is angry.'

'And getting angrier by the day!' added Harry.

'Everyone seems to be grateful to you, Harry, especially the Velvet Lady,' said Louisa.

'Velvet Lady? You mean our new Mayoress? The Velvet Lady is the nickname the children have given her,' explained George. 'Yes, everyone is grateful to Harry.'

'She's very beautiful,' said Louisa, helping herself to a gingerbread biscuit. 'Has she been Mayoress for long?'

'She became Mayoress just after you returned to your world,' said George.

'She's an intelligent woman. Hard-working too. But she tries too hard to please everyone and make her mark on the village,' said Harry.

George jabbed Harry in the ribs with his bony finger. 'That's because she has you to compete with, Harry! I think you've stolen her limelight once too often.'

Louisa felt Jack squirm beside her at the word 'stolen'. Suddenly he leant forwards and blurted out, 'I'm sorry, George. I've done something terrible. I can't hide it any more. We came back because...I took this from you.' He reached into his rucksack and pulled out the leather wallet. 'It's in here.' Checking that no one was watching, he slid the wallet across the table towards George. 'I took it because I thought it would help me. I was curious to find out if the magic would work in our world.'

George glanced around then said in a hushed voice, 'My snowflake?'

Jack nodded. George reached across the table and patted Jack's hand. 'It's all right, my boy. I guessed as much. When I found it was missing from my coat pocket, I thought perhaps you or Louisa had "borrowed" it. Curiosity is a powerful thing, is it not?'

'But I didn't borrow it. I stole it from you. Now it's ruined! The magic didn't help me; it caused chaos! The snowflake has turned a horrible grey colour. I can't clean it! I think I've broken it.'

'We thought perhaps the magic went crazy because we had taken it from the snow globe, away from you where it belongs,' said Louisa.

Harry exchanged a brief glance with George. 'Maybe taking the diamond snowflake from our world has caused the earthquakes,' he said.

Jack's jaw dropped in horror. 'You mean, *I* caused the earthquakes?'

'Don't be alarmed. If it's true, the earthquakes will stop now that you've brought the snowflake back to I-Sing,' George reassured him. He slid the wallet onto his lap. Taking care not to be seen, he peeped inside. 'I thought you said it was ruined?' he whispered. 'It looks perfect to me!'

'What?' cried Jack.

George passed the wallet to Jack and Louisa for them to see. The snowflake was bright and sparkling! 'Returning the snowflake to I-Sing must have restored it,' he said.

'Hopefully its magic is mended, too!' cried Louisa, handing him back the wallet.

'Well done, Jack!' said George. He slipped the wallet into his coat pocket and raised his mug of hot chocolate. 'A toast to Jack. Cheers!'

'Cheers!' said Louisa and Harry, raising their mugs.

For the first time in weeks, Jack smiled.

## Chapter 4

## A New Statue

Louisa was unaware of how long they had been talking until she noticed they were the only ones left in the Great Hall. 'Everyone's gone!' she exclaimed.

'Evening's approaching,' said George, looking through the arched windows at the darkening sky. 'You must stay with me until the snow globe sends you back home.'

Louisa glanced at her watch. 'It can't be evening. It's only one o'clock.'

George slipped a brass watch from his jacket

pocket. 'It's just gone five. You'd best adjust your watch to I-Sing time. You don't want to get in a muddle.'

Louisa fiddled with the buttons on her watch until the screen read 5.05.

'I'd better tidy up this mess!' said Harry, surveying the tables, strewn with dirty crockery and biscuit crumbs. He stretched out a gloved hand. Louisa watched in amazement as the plates and cups washed themselves in a barrel of soapy water that appeared from nowhere. The tables and chairs stacked themselves neatly in a storage cupboard and the doors swung shut behind them.

'Wow!' said Jack.

'Beats washing up 'til midnight,' said Harry as the clean crockery flew into a display case.

'Does it feel as exciting to perform magic with the snowflakes now as it did when you were a boy?' asked Louisa, putting on her coat and rucksack.

'It can make life easier. I know magic is a privilege, but to be honest I'm weary of always being at everyone's beck and call. When I stay with George in the village, people ask for my help day and night, especially since the earthquakes started. I've barely been home to Vorgenhelm. There's always someone who needs a roof repaired, a well unblocked or an animal rescued. I'm glad that I can help people, and I like George's company, but I'm getting too old to be woken at three in the morning!' He adjusted his blue cloak around his bony shoulders with a sigh. 'Ice-Claw, come.'

The spotted snow leopard sprang obediently to his side.

'You should go on a holiday,' suggested Jack.

'I was thinking more of retiring from magic

altogether,' said Harry in a low voice. They left the Great Hall and started to cross the snowy square. 'Perhaps I'll go somewhere warm!' he added as a gust of chilly wind blew snow around them.

Louisa was trying to picture Harry wearing Bermuda shorts and relaxing on a sunny beach when she saw a tarpaulin covering the site where the fountain used to stand. 'What's happened to the fountain?' she asked.

'The Velvet Lady,' said Harry, frowning.

'She's replacing it with a statue of herself,' George explained.

'It should have been finished in time for the Ice Sculpture competition but the building work has been held up by the earthquakes. I have offered to finish it for her,' said Harry, 'but she doesn't want my help. She insists on having it completed by her workmen.'

'Oh no!' gasped Louisa, halting.

'What?' said Jack.

'Don't you remember? When Grandma was transported home with her father, she dropped the diamond snowflake that sends people to other places. It fell into the fountain and was trapped beneath the ice. If workmen have dug up the fountain, they may have found the snowflake!'

'So how will we get back home?' cried Jack.

'Its magic brought you here, so it must still be somewhere in the village,' said George.

'We should search under the tarpaulin,' said Louisa. 'The snowflake could still be there. If someone else finds it, we could be trapped in the snow globe!' She moved towards the fountain.

'Wait!' said Harry.

A group of children ran out of a nearby house to play in the snow.

'We must come back later when we won't be seen.'

Reluctantly, Louisa stopped. 'I guess you're right.'

'This way,' said George. 'We can discuss what to do when we're at home in the warm.'

Louisa recognised the narrow alley that led off the square to George's home. She looked ahead for the familiar blue door. But as they turned the corner, Ice-Claw growled as if sensing danger. The hackles on his neck were raised. George stopped.

A window pane was smashed.

His front door was open, swinging in the breeze.

Someone had got there first…

# Chapter 5
## Break-in

'Stay back!' said Harry, taking the lead. 'Hello? Who's there?' The house was silent. He stepped into the front room. The others followed.

'My poor home!' cried George, scanning the ransacked lounge. The table and chair had been overturned. His other few possessions littered the floor. Louisa stooped to pick up a photograph of George and Harry when they were boys. She handed it to George. 'The glass is cracked but the photo isn't damaged,' she said, trying to sound positive.

'Maybe whoever broke in was looking for something,' said Jack.

'The snowflakes!' groaned Harry, staggering to the kitchen. He let out a cry. Louisa and Jack dashed after him. He was crouching on the floor in front of a little cupboard. The door had been opened with such force that it hung loosely on its hinges.

'The secret compartment!' said Louisa, remembering how George had hidden his diamond snowflake in a concealed section at the back of the cupboard.

'They're gone!' said Harry.

'What's gone?' said Jack.

'The diamond snowflakes.'

'How can they be gone? You've been doing magic all afternoon,' said Louisa, 'Surely you're wearing the snowflakes?'

'No,' said Harry. 'Only these two.' He slipped off his gloves to reveal two diamond snowflakes, one on each palm. 'I need to touch the snowflakes for the magic to work. I realised some months ago that having them around my neck was too risky. Someone was bound to notice what I was doing.'

'I told him his cloak was too loose and flappy! It wasn't the ideal way to hide the diamonds!' said George.

'I chose the two snowflakes that I was most likely to need – one that creates objects and one that controls the movement of objects. I thought I could keep them hidden inside my gloves. Then, when I perform magic, it looks completely natural,' said Harry.

'I suggested that he hid the remaining seven in here,' George explained. 'As you know, Louisa, it's where I kept my diamond snowflake safe for years before I lent it to you. I thought it was for the best. This is all my fault!'

'Nonsense!' said Harry. 'You can't blame yourself. For some time I've felt as though someone is watching me – and following me. I've seen movements in the shadows, and heard strange noises at night. I agreed that hiding the snowflakes here was the safest option.'

'But why all the secrecy?' asked Jack. 'Does it matter if the villagers know that it's the snowflakes that give you your magical powers, Harry?'

'Yes,' cried Louisa. 'Because then someone might want to steal them to use the magic for themselves!'

'Such power in the wrong hands...' George's voice trailed off.

'What we dreaded most has now happened.' Harry sighed.

Jack glanced at Ice-Claw, who was sniffing the ground as if hunting for clues. 'What about Ice-Claw? I thought you needed the snowflake that controls animals to make him obedient to you?'

'At first, yes. But I've trained him for so long that he's learned to listen to me without magic.'

Jack backed away from the great cat. 'So Ice-Claw isn't under magical control?'

Harry shook his head. 'At least I can still help you clear up the mess, George.' He folded his fingers around the diamond in his right hand.

The chair righted itself, and a clock and vase lying on the floor returned to their place on mantelpiece. Scattered books flew onto the bookcase. Fragments of glass from the broken window rose from the rug and joined together in the air, forming a smooth pane which glided towards the window. As it did, something blue, red and green fluttered in the frame.

'What's that?' said Louisa, crossing the room. Snagged on the wooden frame was a

fragment of rainbow-coloured cloth. She tugged it free and showed the others.

'How did it get there?' puzzled George, peering at the torn fabric through his spectacles.

'Whoever broke the glass to undo the latch must have caught their sleeve on the frame,' said Harry.

'We've seen that material before,' said Jack to Louisa. 'Don't you remember? That strange man trying to sell us stuff. His coat was colourful like this!'

'The pedlar?' questioned George. 'That menace! He's been in the village for some time, pestering us all to buy his wares.'

'Could he be the one who has been spying on you, Harry?' said Jack.

'I suppose so. He came from Port Marinna about a fortnight ago. He's been staying at the inn in the square. It would be easy for him to spy on me, living so close. The timings fit, too.'

'Then we've got to find him!' said Louisa. 'We can't let him get away with your diamond snowflakes!'

George's jaw dropped. 'What's happened to timid Louisa?'

Harry rubbed his wrinkled forehead and sank into the armchair. 'I'm sorry. I haven't the energy to go chasing thieves.'

Ice-Claw licked his master's hand and gave a gruff meow.

'We need to hurry before the pedlar leaves the village,' said Jack. 'We'll go, won't we, Louisa?'

Louisa found herself nodding. George was right. She wasn't the same timid girl who had been terrified of journeying to the Miser's castle when they were last in the snow globe. 'When you've climbed a mountain and overcome a magical Miser, nothing seems as frightening!' she said.

Harry chuckled.

'Can you show us the way to the inn, George? Maybe the pedlar is still there,' said Jack.

George unhooked a lantern from the wall. 'Or course,' he replied. 'Come on, you two. We've got a thief to catch!'

## Chapter 6
## Escape

Jack and Louisa followed George along the street that led to the square. Lights from the bustling inn shone across the snow. Through the window they could see rosy-cheeked men laughing as they drank from tankards.

'Stay here,' said George. 'I'll speak to the innkeeper.'

Jack and Louisa watched as George weaved his way through the crowd and spoke to a plump woman behind the bar. They saw her scowl, then shake her head. Moments later,

George returned. 'He's gone. The landlady found his room empty this afternoon. He left without paying his bill.'

'No wonder she looks cross!' said Jack.

'Then we've missed him!' said Louisa. 'Now where do we search?'

George's bushy eyebrows knotted in a frown. 'My guess is that he will head for Port Marinna. Husky sledges run regularly to the port from an outpost at the edge of the village.'

'If he reaches the port before we find him, he could sail anywhere,' said Jack.

'Then we'll never catch him or find the diamond snowflakes!' cried Louisa.

Jack took a deep breath. 'We must go at once!'

Louisa recognised the wild look in Jack's green eyes. They gleamed with the same thirst for adventure that she had seen when he had volunteered to find the Miser and rescue the villagers' voices.

George shook his head. 'It's at least two days' journey to Port Marinna. I haven't the stamina to come with you. I can't send you off by yourselves!'

'We've done it before,' said Jack, grinning. 'Besides, we've come prepared this time!' He patted his rucksack, strapped to his back.

'We could borrow your snowflake again. It will help if we get into trouble,' said Louisa.

George's grey eyes clouded with concern. 'I don't like you going. But I can't stop you. Promise that if it gets too dangerous, you will come back. You're more important than magical diamonds!' He handed her the wallet containing the snowflake.

Louisa flung her arms around the elderly man's neck. 'We promise. Don't worry. Your snowflake will look after us, just as it did last time.'

'I'll walk you to the edge of the village. You need to follow Portland Road. It's the only route that leads from the village to Port Marinna. It runs parallel to the river. Here, you take the lantern, Louisa.'

As they trudged across the square, they passed the site where the fountain was being dismantled and rebuilt. Louisa stopped. She glanced around then ducked beneath the tarpaulin.

'Hey, what are you doing?' asked Jack.

'Getting all the help we can!' she said. 'Keep watch!'

'Someone from the inn might see you,' said George.

Jack fidgeted nervously. 'We don't have time for this.'

'If the snowflake is buried here, we ought to get it now, before the workmen find it!' Louisa hissed. 'This might be our only chance.'

Before Jack could reply, a guard in a green velvet uniform strode towards them.

'Louisa! Get out!' cried Jack, lifting the sheeting.

'Halt!' barked the guard in a voice as rough as gravel.

Louisa emerged. The evening shadows played on the guard's face as he stormed towards them. With his drooping ginger moustache and bulging cheeks, he looked like an angry walrus. 'That's private property!' he barked.

Louisa's insides quivered as he towered over her.

'Good evening, Gustav,' said George graciously, stepping between them and leaning on his stick. 'May we help you?'

'What are you playing at under there?' spat the guard, brushing George aside.

'Nothing, sir, really...' stammered Louisa.

'Nothing, hey? Looks like sabotage! Come with me at once! You'll have to answer to the Mayoress!' Gustav took Louisa by the elbow, squeezing it with his fat fingers.

She wriggled in his grip, and dropped the lantern.

'No!' yelled Jack, pulling at the guard.

Louisa twisted free. She turned to George. He mouthed a single word to her.

'RUN!'

## Chapter 7
## On the Run

Jack grabbed Louisa's hand and pulled her away.

'We can't leave George!' she cried.

'We must!'

Louisa stumbled in the thick snow. The guard blew his whistle, calling for help. Glancing back, she saw a second guard running to the scene. He was completely bald and built like an SAS soldier. Gustav gabbled something to him then pointed in their direction. Immediately the guard started to sprint towards them.

'There's another guard! He's chasing us!' Louisa wailed.

'Portland Road!' cried Jack, seeing a sign and veering to the left. 'Over here!'

They turned down a street that sloped away from the square. Louisa glimpsed the guard over her shoulder. 'He's getting closer! We'll have to hide!'

'In here!' cried Jack, ducking behind a log pile at the back of a chalet.

Louisa dropped beside him. 'He'll easily find us here,' she panicked.

'We can't outrun him,' panted Jack.

Louisa tried to ignore the cobwebs that fluttered between the logs next to her. She crouched as low as she could. As she did, the diamond in her pocket jabbed into her tummy. 'Of course! The snowflake!' She reached into her pocket and clasped the diamond. 'Help!

Don't let us be seen!' she murmured. She felt Jack move beside her. She opened her eyes. Jack had vanished. 'Jack, where are you?' she whispered.

'I'm right here!'

Louisa saw a puff of breath appear from nowhere. 'I can't see you!'

'I can't see you either. We're invisible!'

Louisa looked down at her coat – or, at least, where her coat should have been. She found herself gaping straight through her body at the snow on the ground.

'How cool is this?' said Jack.

'Shhh!'

They heard the muffled *thud, thud* of the guard's boots as he grew closer. He stopped a few metres away, breathing hard.

'I know you're here!' he called. He paused as if listening for any sign of movement.

Louisa and Jack kept perfectly still. He glanced towards the log pile, staring straight at them. Louisa held her breath. Seeing nothing, he moved further down the street.

After several minutes had passed, Jack whispered, 'I think it's safe to move.'

'We should stay away from the main street,' said Louisa. 'I don't want to run into that guard again. We're not so invisible any more!' She stared at her ghostly limbs as they gradually reappeared.

'How do we reach Port Marinna if we can't use the road?' asked Jack.

'Didn't George say something about a river?' Louisa answered.

'That's right! He said the road ran parallel to the river.'

'That's it! All rivers lead to the sea. If we follow the river, it should lead us to the port!'

'We can avoid the main road. The guard won't find us,' said Jack. 'Louisa, you're a genius!'

'Not really. I just paid attention in geography!'

They crept from their hiding place. A thick pine forest ran behind the row of chalets. 'I'm glad there are plenty of trees,' said Louisa. 'It'll make it easier to stay out of sight.'

'Let's head away from the village to the left. That's where we'll find the river,' said Jack.

'Yes, but we should keep moving downhill too,' said Louisa.

They tramped through the thick snow, weaving their way in the gloom between the tall pine trees. 'I hate the dark!' said Louisa, stopping and searching through her rucksack. 'Hang on, Jack. I packed my torch somewhere.'

'No. The guard might see the light. We can't

risk attracting his attention,' said Jack. 'Put it away.'

'Bossy boots,' Louisa huffed under her breath.

Jack trudged onwards. 'At least the snow reflects the moonlight enough for us see where we're going.'

'I suppose.' Louisa sighed and zipped up her bag. 'I just keep imagining wild animals or angry guards hiding in every shadow, ready to leap out at us!'

'You sound like the old timid Louisa. What happened to the "I can do anything" Louisa?'

'That Louisa prefers street lights!'

They walked on in silence, moving in a diagonal line away from the village.

'We must have walked for miles,' said Louisa at last. 'I hope we find the river soon. I'd hate to get lost in these woods.'

'I know,' said Jack.

Louisa's feet ached. 'Do you think the guard is still searching for us? We've been walking for ages. I bet he's given up. Gone back to I-Sing.'

'I hope he's turned back,' said Jack. He staggered slightly in a deep patch of snow. 'We

must keep moving. The pedlar already has a couple of hours' head start on us. Every minute we stop, he's getting closer to the port, and our chance of stopping him escaping with the snowflakes becomes slimmer.'

They continued for another half an hour, when Jack suddenly stopped. 'Hey! Look down here!' He pointed to a shallow bank that sloped downwards to a wide, flat stretch of snow that snaked its way between the trees. 'We've found the river!'

'Don't tell me – ice?' groaned Louisa, remembering the time she had slipped through the frozen moat when they were last in the snow globe.

'We don't have to cross it, just follow it! Come on!' Jack led the way along the line of the river. At times they had to detour around bushes or scramble over boulders that blocked the way.

They had been following the riverbank for over an hour when Louisa heard a familiar gurgling. 'Your poor tummy, Jack. I can hear it from here! I'm hungry too. Let's eat something.'

Jack halted. 'Er...'

'What's wrong?'

'I got peckish earlier and ate my ration when we were walking to George's house.'

'What?' cried Louisa. 'You said you'd packed extra.'

'I'm a growing boy!'

'We have at a two-day journey ahead of us and you have no food?'

'If we had Harry's diamond snowflake, we could make all the food we need!' Jack sulked. 'Roast chicken, sausage rolls, pizza, that chocolate pudding that Grandma makes...'

'Stop it, Jack. That doesn't help. You'll have to share mine.' Louisa pulled a cereal bar from her rucksack and passed a small chunk to Jack.

'Is that all?'

'It's more than you deserve!' Louisa stomped ahead, chewing the rest of the bar. She hadn't gone far when her foot caught on a piece of wood buried in the snow. 'Argh!' she cried, falling onto her hands and knees.

'Are you all right?' asked Jack, stooping beside her. 'Looks like you tripped on a bit of broken fence.' He waggled a line of rickety fence panels to her right.

'I'm fine. Fencing? Out here? Why would someone...' She stood up. Outlined against the moonlit snow was a small, dilapidated chalet.

'Do you think someone is living there?' whispered Louisa. 'Maybe they have food and could help us.'

'There's only one way to find out,' said Jack. 'Come on!'

## Chapter 8
## In the Shadows

They drew closer to the chalet. The weather-beaten panels were cracked. A ragged curtain fluttered through a broken window. Jack banged on the front door. The broken latch gave way and the door opened. He called into the darkness, 'Hello! Anyone home?'

The only reply was the sigh of the breeze.

'There's no one here,' said Louisa. 'Please, let's go. It's giving me the creeps!'

'Just a minute,' said Jack, disappearing into the murky shack.

Louisa could hear the floorboards groaning under his weight. 'Be careful! I'll get my torch.'

'It's fine.' No sooner than had Jack spoken, Louisa heard a dull snap, followed by a thump.

'Ow!'

'Jack?' Louisa pulled out her torch. Its beam caught Jack. He lay crumpled on the floor. 'Are you okay?'

'I'm fine. It's just a rotten floorboard. My foot went through.'

'Are you hurt?'

Jack pulled his boot free. 'Nah. It just gave me a fright.'

Louisa shone her torch around the room. 'We should take a look around. There might be something useful here.'

'This looks like the only room. There's a cooking area at that end,' said Jack. He stepped carefully towards a log-burning stove and a couple of dirty cupboards. He looked inside. 'There's nothing here. Just a few rags.'

'It's a shame there's no furniture except for that,' said Louisa, pointing to a padded bench fixed along one wall. 'It's not much, but we could shelter here for a bit.'

'I don't want to stop,' said Jack.

'Well, we'll travel quicker once we've rested. Besides, the pedlar will have to sleep too. It's better sleeping in here than on the mountain.'

Jack shivered. 'Shame we don't have a blanket or something. It's freezing!'

'Actually, we do. I packed our sleeping bags!' said Louisa.

'You're amazing! I don't suppose you have any extra food, too?'

Louisa scowled and threw a sleeping bag at him. She pushed the front door shut as best as she could to keep out the wind. 'Pass me those rags. I can use them to block the cold air coming through the broken window.'

Jack fished the rags out from the cupboard and tossed them to her. She caught them and made her way towards the window, testing each floorboard with her toe to ensure it was solid before putting her weight on it. Suddenly she heard the scuffling of tiny paws. Something darted out of the shadows and scuttled over her boot. She screamed and leapt onto the bench, dropping the torch.

'It's only a mouse!' said Jack. 'There are probably loads in an old house like this.'

'That's not comforting!' gasped Louisa.

Jack picked up her torch. He shone it under the bench and swung its beam around the room. 'It's gone. You can jump down.'

'There's no way I'm touching the floor again tonight! I'm staying on this bench!' She shuffled

along the the padded cushion and stuffed the rags into the hole in the window.

'I'll set my alarm.' Jack adjusted his watch, then snuggled inside his sleeping bag.

Louisa cast a wary glance around the room. She yanked off her boots and wriggled, fully clothed, into her sleeping bag. The bench smelt of dogs and dirt. Her skin prickled as she lay down, knowing that mice might be living a few centimetres away. She used her rucksack as a pillow and tried to get comfortable.

Jack yawned. 'Get some sleep. See you in a few hours.'

Louisa's mind filled with images of mice scuttling from every crack in the house, swarming over her. She pulled the sleeping bag over her head. She imagined herself curled up under her soft duvet at home, safe and warm. At last, she fell asleep...

She woke to the beeping of Jack's alarm. Outside it was still dark. She flicked on her torch. Jack had rolled off the bench in the night and lay on the floor, snoring. Louisa giggled. He often thrashed about in his sleep. At least he hadn't sleep-walked as he sometimes did. 'Jack! It's time to get up!'

As Jack stirred, Louisa realised that the snoring was not coming from him at all. She listened hard, her heart galloping. The laboured breathing came from the other side of the front door. 'Jack!' she hissed, prodding him with her foot.

The nasal sound became more like a growl. 'Jack!' She shook him awake. 'We're not alone! There's something at the door!'

Jack sat up and rubbed his eyes. He heard the snoring and sprang to his feet. Nearby was a piece of loose floorboard. He prised it up with his fingers and brandished it like a weapon. Louisa shone the torch at the doorway. Claws scraped against the door. Suddenly, it swung open...

# Chapter 9
## A Gift

Into the room bounded a huge spotted creature. Louisa screamed. Jack went to strike the animal with the floorboard. The beast crouched in defence, glaring at him with piercing blue eyes. It bared his fangs and snarled. Louisa stared at the speckled face. 'Ice-Claw?'

The big cat relaxed his jaw. His eyes softened and he gave a gentle meow.

'Ice-Claw, it is you!' Louisa exclaimed.

Jack lowered his weapon. 'What's he doing here?'

Ice-Claw padded over to Louisa and lifted his chin. Hanging from a strap tied around his neck was a leather pouch. 'I think he wants me to take the pouch!' she said. 'Harry must have sent him.'

Jack backed away. 'Is he safe?'

Ice-Claw swished his long bushy tail, keeping his chin raised, waiting for Louisa to remove the pouch. Louisa knelt to untie it. 'He seems safe.' The snow leopard nuzzled his head against her coat. 'See?'

Jack relaxed. 'I wonder why he was so aggressive at first?'

'Probably because you were about to hit him with a plank of wood!' said Louisa.

Jack flung the plank aside. 'Sorry, Ice-Claw. What's in the pouch?'

Louisa took it from Ice-Claw's neck. Inside were two diamond snowflakes and a note.

To my dearest Louisa and Jack,
I seem to have got you into another fix!
I am sorry I cannot be of greater help.
Remain watchful. The guards seem
determined to find you. They have been
here asking questions. Be of good courage –
you are more than fit for the task!
Harry has instructed Ice-Claw to give you
the enclosed gift. May they serve you well.
All my love, Your Friend, George

'Well done, Ice-Claw. You brought us Harry's snowflakes!' cried Louisa.

Ice-Claw padded towards the door.

'You know what this means, don't you?' said Jack, grinning and taking the diamond snowflakes from Louisa. 'Breakfast!'

'What about Ice-Claw?' Louisa patted her knees. 'Here, boy!'

'He's not a dog!' said Jack.

Ice-claw meowed gruffly. He nudged the door aside with his nose and gave them one last glance before disappearing into the forest.

Louisa darted after him. 'No! Come back!'

'Let him go,' called Jack. 'We can't force him to stay. He's probably going back to Harry.'

Louisa stood on the porch, staring into the forest. 'I wanted him to stay. I feel safer having an animal with us. Especially if George is right and the guards are still searching for us.'

'Ice-Claw didn't make me feel very safe!' said Jack.

Louisa fiddled with the snowflake in her pocket. 'I miss Daisy. Such a kind, brave horse. It was so good of her owner to lend her to us last time. I wish we had an animal to help us.'

'I don't miss getting saddle-sore and a numb bum!' Jack grimaced. 'There's nothing we can do about Ice-Claw. He's done his job. He's brought us the diamond snowflakes.'

'I suppose.'

'Come on, I'm starving! I wonder what I can make for breakfast with the magic? Which snowflake do you suppose creates objects?'

In the torchlight, Louisa examined the diamond snowflakes. 'The patterns are different. This one has a ring of triangles in the middle. That one has a ring of teardrops.'

'Oh, yeah!' said Jack. 'But which one creates objects?'

'Try asking the triangle one for food.'

Jack held the triangle-patterned snowflake in his right hand. 'Give us two bacon rolls and two spiced buns.'

The food appeared in Jack's hands, wrapped in a cloth. 'It worked!' he cried. The salty smell of bacon wafted into the cabin.

Louisa frowned. 'You know I don't like bacon.'

'Sorry. I forgot. Never mind – more for me!' He slid the bacon from her roll and added it to his.

Louisa glared at him.

Jack paused mid-chew and sighed. 'Give us jam and apple juice,' he told the diamond.

A mini pot of jam and a jug of juice appeared on the floor. 'Better?'

Louisa grinned. 'Much.' She spread the jam with her finger. 'I suppose the other snowflake must have the power to move objects,' she said.

'Yeah! I'll try,' said Jack. He held the diamond with the teardrop pattern in one hand and fixed his attention on his bacon roll in the other. The roll lifted off his hand and glided towards his mouth. 'It's working!' he cried, then *wumph*! The bun smacked into his forehead, missing his mouth, and fell into his lap.

'Harder than it looks, eh?' Louisa teased.

'Just need a little practice.' Jack wiped off the sauce from his face with his sleeve and tucked the diamonds back into the leather pouch. When they had finished breakfast, they packed their rucksacks and made their way to the river. 'Shouldn't it be getting light by now?' asked Louisa, using her torch to navigate through the trees.

'It's still very early,' said Jack.

Suddenly there was a flash of white. Something darted through the trees to their left.

'What was that?' asked Louisa, the hairs on her neck standing on end.

'What?'

'I saw something move. Something white – in the trees.'

'Ice-Claw?'

'No. It was too big.'

Jack scanned the forest. 'Maybe you imagined it.'

Louisa kicked the snow. 'I didn't imagine it. You never believe me! Just because I'm younger than you...'

'It's not because you're younger. I can't see anything. I don't think there's anything there.'

Louisa huffed and followed him along the riverbank. 'I wonder if we could find a quicker way of reaching the port instead of walking. We should use the diamond snowflakes. We could ask the triangle snowflake to create skis or a snowmobile!'

'Neither of us can ski. And remember, we can only create objects that already exist in the snow globe world. From what Grandma told us, engines haven't been invented here.'

'There must be something else to make us travel faster. George said that the pedlar is probably travelling by husky sledge. Ask for a husky sledge.'

'We don't have any huskies.'

'Then create some!' Louisa huffed.

Jack held the diamond snowflake that had the triangle pattern. 'Give us a team of husky dogs.'

Nothing happened.

'See? The snowflake creates *objects,* not *animals,*' said Jack.

'Then ask for a normal sledge! The mountain is steep enough to sledge down to the port.'

'I suppose.' Jack shrugged.

'I'm sure it will work. The forest isn't as thick here.'

'Still, it'll be tricky dodging the trees,' said Jack.

'Urgh! Can't you accept any of my ideas?'

Jack sighed. 'All right. We can try. Give us two sledges.'

At once, two wooden sledges appeared in the snow.

'Wow!' said Louisa. 'They're not like our plastic sledges at home. They look like something from a history book!' She sat on the nearest sledge and picked up the rope. She tucked her feet onto the runners and pushed off. The sledge slid forwards, gradually gaining speed. The wind rushed at her face, making her cheeks smart. 'How do we steer these things?'

'Dig your heels into the snow,' called Jack. 'Like this!'

Louisa could hear Jack's sledge swooshing through the snow behind her. She craned her neck to see how Jack was steering. 'I can't see your feet. It's too dark!'

'Louisa! Watch out! The tree!'

Louisa whipped her head around. Her sledge was hurtling straight for a tree. She thrust her heels into the snow. A shower of snow sprayed into her face like shards of ice. She forced her heels deeper in the snow, but was travelling too fast to stop.

'Louisa!' cried Jack.

Louisa shoved her hand into her pocket and grabbed George's diamond. 'Help us!' she cried.

Immediately she felt the sledge veer to the left. It skimmed past the tree, missing it by a whisker. She gripped the rope. The sledge continued to increase in speed. 'You okay, Jack?' she gasped.

'Yes! But I'm not in control of this thing. It's steering itself!' he called.

'Mine too! It's magic!' Louisa gazed at her sledge. The wooden frame glowed with a silver

light as it flashed past the trees. Silver sparks flew from the runners. Faster and faster the sledge raced down the mountain, swerving around trees, reaching a terrifying speed. Louisa sat rigid with fear. Suddenly, the sledge struck a bump in the snow. It flew into the air like a skateboard taking off from a ramp. A scream caught in Louisa's throat. She clung on to the sledge, expecting to be catapulted from it at any moment. Instead, the sledge glided back to the ground.

'This is incredible!' she cried. The mountainside become more level. The sledge slowed down. Eventually it scraped to a halt. She tried nudging it forwards with her heels. Her legs ached with the effort, and the sledge barely moved. The silver colour faded from the frame.

Jack's sledge drew to a standstill beside her. 'That was awesome! It's a shame we stopped.'

Louisa dug her feet into the snow. 'I'm trying to get moving again but...urgh! The sledge won't budge!' Just then, something caught Louisa's attention on the path ahead. 'Jack! Look over there. We're being watched!'

## Chapter 10
## Creeping Darkness

The dull morning sun shone on a creature the size of a small pony with a long snout and oversized ears. He was standing further along the riverbank, staring at them with large brown eyes.

'What is it?' whispered Louisa. 'A deer?'

'I think it's a baby moose.'

'What's that dangly thing under his chin?'

'Dunno. It's just how he's made.'

The moose twitched his nose and blinked.

'He's cute!' said Louisa, edging towards

him. 'There, there, good boy.' She reached out to stroke his neck. The moose gave a soft snort and sniffed her glove.

Jack fidgeted. 'Louisa, I don't think that's a good idea...'

Suddenly there was a loud grunt behind them. Louisa spun around. From the trees strode

an enormous adult moose. Louisa felt her legs turn to water. The huge creature glared at her. The whites of its eyes flashed and it lowered its head, ready to charge.

'Hey! Over here!' yelled Jack, waving his arms.

The beast turned its great head in his direction.

'Louisa, run!' Jack shouted.

Louisa stumbled away from the baby. The adult moose saw her move. It snorted, then charged at her. Panic seized Louisa's lungs, paralysing her. She tried to run, but her legs wouldn't move. She clenched the snowflake in her pocket and gasped, 'Help!'

From within the forest, a deep animal cry rang out like the bellowing of a bull. The adult moose halted. It threw back its head and listened. The cry echoed through the trees again. The baby moose scurried to the adult's side. Together, they turned and trotted into the woods, vanishing among the trees.

Louisa sank to the ground, trembling.

Jack raced to her side. 'You okay?'

'I just need to catch my breath.'

'I thought it was going to kill you!'

'Me too! What frightened it away?'

'It was that weird noise. It sounded like a cow. I don't think it frightened the moose. Whatever it was, it seemed to be calling to her.'

'Her? The moose was a female?'

'I guess so. It must have been the mother. Mothers will do anything to protect their young.' He took Louisa's hand and helped her up.

Louisa brushed the snow off her jeans. 'I shouldn't have tried to stroke the baby. Stupid of me.'

Jack didn't answer. He was staring straight over her head, looking at the sky. 'What on earth—'

Louisa followed his gaze. A massive black cloud was moving towards them. 'Is it a storm cloud?'

'I've never seen anything like it. It's so thick and black. It can't just be a rain cloud. It looks all wrong.'

'It doesn't feel normal,' Louisa murmured. 'It's as if there's something sinister in the air.'

'Let's get moving. The sledges are no good to us now. The ground is too flat here.' Jack marched ahead, keeping parallel to the river.

Before Louisa could catch up with him, the ground trembled. The mountain groaned like a bear with tummy ache. It lasted a few seconds then stopped. 'What was that?' gasped Louisa. 'Another earthquake?'

'But surely that's impossible!' said Jack. 'The snowflakes are all inside the snow globe. Harry said everything would be all right now that we've brought George's snowflake back!'

Louisa gazed at the thick black mass in the sky floating steadily towards them. She took the diamond snowflake from her pocket. It was covered with grey flecks. She rubbed it with her glove. It remained dull and dirty. 'Jack! The snowflake is going bad again!'

Jack jogged to her side. 'Let me see!' His mouth gaped open. 'How could this happen?' He took out the leather pouch that Harry had sent with Ice-Claw. 'These are going grey too!'

Louisa gazed mournfully at the diamonds. 'Their magic is going all wrong. Maybe they've caused the black cloud. Maybe it's because the diamond snowflakes don't just belong in the snow globe – they belong in I-Sing with Harry!

We're taking them further and further away from their home.'

'And so is the pedlar,' said Jack. 'The black cloud is coming from the south – from Port Marinna.'

'Maybe the pedlar has already reached the port?'

'Perhaps. We've got to hurry. We have to find him and return the snowflakes to Harry before there are more earthquakes. If we don't, I-Sing could be...'

'...destroyed!'

# Chapter 11
## Rapids

Jack stood on the bank scratching his head. 'We've got to find a quick way to reach the port.'

Louisa's eyes followed the winding river. 'What about a rowing boat?'

'The river is frozen!' said Jack.

'We could slide on the ice. We could use the paddles to push ourselves along. It would be faster than walking. In a boat we won't sink if the ice breaks!'

'It's a crazy idea!'

'Have you got a better one?'

Jack shook his head. He held the diamond snowflake with the triangle pattern towards the river. 'Give us a rowing boat!'

For several seconds nothing happened, then a rowing boat appeared on the ice. 'Phew! The magic worked!' he said, picking up the mooring rope that lay at his feet. 'I was worried that the snowflake might malfunction and give us an igloo or something crazy.'

'It has malfunctioned! Look – those are snow shovels, not paddles!' said Louisa, pointing at the stern where two shovels lay.

'Well, we'll have to do what we can with them. Jump in. I'll hold the boat steady.'

Louisa didn't move. She stood, staring at the ice, feeling the colour drain from her face. 'Maybe this wasn't such a good idea.'

'You won't fall through the ice again,' said

Jack. 'You'll be safe in the boat. You said so yourself. Come on, we have to do this!'

Louisa pushed the memory of plunging into freezing water out of her mind. She pictured Harry and George, shaken by the earthquake. I-Sing needed her help. She skittered down the bank and climbed into the boat. Jack sat beside her. He used a shovel to push away from the bank. The boat slid across the river like an ice hockey puck. 'We need to push against the ice at the same time to move in a straight line,' he said.

At first, the boat was difficult to manoeuvre. The slightest change in the way they positioned the shovels sent it careering off-course. Louisa's muscles throbbed. Sweat beaded on her brow. 'This is so hard!' she groaned.

'We're moving at a good speed,' said Jack. 'Keep going!'

After a clumsy start, they settled into a rhythm. Above, the menacing black cloud had taken over almost the entire sky. 'I don't like how dark it's getting,' said Louisa. She checked the time. 'It's supposed to be midday. Instead it feels like midnight! My body doesn't know what to feel – whether to eat lunch or go to bed!'

Jack grinned. 'Eat. Always choose food.'

'You would say that! I wish it was lighter, so we could see where we're going.'

'At least travelling on the river means we can't get lost. This river has to lead to the sea and the port,' said Jack.

'I wonder what happens to the ice when we reach the sea? I suppose it must break up – unless the sea is frozen too.' Louisa's tummy bundled into a knot. She focused on the ice ahead. Under the oppressive black cloud, she could just make out the white ice. They slid along in silence for what seemed like a lifetime – until suddenly they heard a crack beneath the boat. Louisa's heart flipped. On either side of them, the ice shattered. The bow of the boat plunged downwards. Water sloshed against the panels.

Louisa shut her eyes. The boat bobbed back up then settled on the surface.

'We're floating!' said Jack.

Louisa opened her eyes. Sure enough, the water was calm. The boat was drifting along peacefully with the current. Louisa laughed with relief. 'I can't believe we're safe! Maybe George's snowflake helped.' She took the diamond snowflake from her pocket. Her laughter died away. 'Oh Jack, look at the snowflake! It's turning black!'

He leant across to see. 'It must be getting more damaged the further we take it from I-Sing.'

'So the snowflake didn't help us just now when the ice broke?'

'I don't think so. Not if it's going black like this. Remember what I told you about using it back at home? It caused chaos. We can't trust it!'

'What about your diamond snowflakes, Jack? They might have gone bad too! Check them!'

Jack balanced his shovel across his knees. He took the pouch from his pocket and inspected the diamonds. Even in the dim light, he could see that they were covered in black blotches. 'We can't rely on their magic to help us now. We mustn't touch them!' He thrust the leather pouch at arm's length as if it contained deadly poison.

Louisa took it from him. 'I'll carry it if you're afraid of the snowflakes.' She put her diamond snowflake inside with the other two, and stuffed the pouch into her pocket.

'I'm not *afraid*,' he protested. 'It's just that I've experienced the mayhem they can cause.' He picked up his shovel and focused on guiding the boat.

The current was stronger now and swept the boat along with some speed. 'This is better,' said Louisa. 'We'll get to the port much quicker.'

Just then they heard galloping hooves thudding along the riverbank. Louisa looked across. A streak of white flashed before them, then faded into the darkness as it raced ahead.

'What was that?' asked Jack.

'It looks like the same white flicker I saw in the woods yesterday. And earlier today!' said Louisa. 'Could it be Daisy?'

'I doubt it.'

Louisa scowled. Her thoughts raced. *Maybe Daisy has come to help us? Perhaps I'll ride her again!* She was imagining cantering on Daisy through the snow when the boat struck something hard. It lurched sideways, causing Louisa to drop her shovel. She fumbled in the bottom of the boat to find it.

The river grew choppy. The boat surged forwards, propelled by a powerful current. 'Whoa!' yelled Jack. 'Rapids!'

Louisa leant backwards, holding tightly to the bench. The small vessel bashed into boulders as it plunged down the river. Icy water sprayed over the sides of the boat. 'Jack! Do something!' Louisa screamed, terrified that their little boat would shatter into pieces.

'I am doing something! I'm holding on!' he yelled. His shovel flipped into the rushing water as he clung to the side.

The boat hit a huge boulder, tipping it sideways. The wood groaned under the strain. A crack appeared in the front panel. 'It's breaking up!' cried Louisa.

Suddenly there was an animal cry from further along the river. It was followed by a series of grunts then the sound of splitting wood, as if a tree trunk had been snapped.

The current swept the boat around a sharp bend in the river, smashing it against a rock. The damaged panel gave way. Water gushed into the boat. Louisa looked up just in time to see a fallen pine tree spanning the river like a bridge in front of them. 'Jump!' she yelled.

They threw themselves out of the sinking boat and grabbed the tree's spiky branches. Shaking with fear, they clung on as the raging river rushed beneath them. 'Climb along the tree towards the bank,' shouted Jack.

Louisa was gripping a branch so tightly that she was unable to move. 'I can't! I'll fall!'

'You have to! Remember when you last climbed a tree? Move your hands a bit at a time. Find a secure place to put your feet.'

Louisa shuffled along the tree, inching towards the bank.

'Keep going! You're doing really well!'

At last, solid ground was within reach. She let go and jumped, landing safely. Behind her the tree jolted, slipping further into the river. Jack lost his footing and slipped. He grabbed at the branch, his feet dangling in the water.

'Jack!' She reached towards him.

He swung his legs, trying to gain a foothold. The tree sank lower. Water washed over his feet. Louisa reached for his hand. 'I'll help you!' she cried.

Jack launched himself towards the bank as Louisa pulled him. He landed on the bank just as the tree slid into the water and was swept away by the current.

They lay in the snow, panting for breath. 'That was close!' gasped Louisa.

'We're lucky that tree was blocking the river,' said Jack.

'I know!' Louisa replayed the scene in her mind. 'I heard a weird cracking sound before we came around the corner. Maybe that was the tree splitting.'

'I heard that too. I wonder what caused the tree to fall?'

'There was a strange animal noise just before. Perhaps an animal pushed the tree over?'

'I guess it's possible,' Jack mused, sitting up. 'Why would it do that?'

'It could have been that white thing that galloped past us. Maybe it went ahead of us and pushed the tree across the river. Perhaps it was trying to help us. It could have been Daisy! Can a horse push a tree over?'

'Doubt it. But whatever it was, I'm grateful it came to our rescue.'

Louisa tried to stand. Her legs wobbled. 'I need some food.' She took a chocolate bar, a packet of crisps and a water bottle from her bag and shared them with Jack.

'That's better,' she said when they had finished.

They rested long enough to recover their strength then continued to walk along the riverbank. After half an hour, Jack stopped and pointed ahead of them. 'See that yellowish light?'

'Yes. It looks like the glow of street lights,' said Louisa.

'We must be close to the port!' said Jack. 'Come on! We're almost there!'

# Chapter 12
## Port Marinna

Jack and Louisa jogged along the riverbank, their breath forming white puffs as they ran. 'The air smells salty. Like the sea,' panted Louisa. 'We're close!'

'Yes! Look ahead!' said Jack.

Out of the darkness, a row of chalets appeared. 'They're just like the ones in I-Sing,' said Louisa. 'And look at the river.'

They peered to their left. Replacing the sloping riverbank was a vertical wall. Louisa grinned. 'Can you hear that?' They leant over

the edge and could hear the *slosh, slap* of waves lapping against stone. 'It's the sea.'

'This wall must be part of the harbour. Come on,' cried Jack. He followed the wall as it curved to the right. They rounded a bend and stopped dead in their tracks. Rows of sailing ship masts reached up into the sky. The tackle clanked as the boats rocked in the harbour.

'Wow! Sailing ships!' breathed Jack.

Louisa gazed in awe at them. 'Just like on TV!'

Wooden jetties ran from the harbour alongside each ship. Sitting on barrels along the length of the dock were merchants in fine suits, sailors wearing blue hats and fishermen in oilskin jackets. They huddled around fires lit in iron stands.

'How can they bear to sit outside in the snow? It's freezing, even with the fires!' said Louisa, shivering.

'Shouldn't they be working?' said Jack.

A wrinkled old man resting on the harbour wall called out to them. 'It be that cloud there.' He jabbed his pipe towards the sky. 'No one dares set out to sea with that menace hanging over us. Never seen a darkness like it. Middle of the day and it's black as night!'

'Some awful mischief is brewing,' chirped a skinny sailor nearby. He shifted his weight nervously from foot to foot, his eyes wide with fear. 'No sailor would set out to sea with that hanging over them!'

'Aye,' croaked the man with the pipe. 'No ship has left the harbour all morning.'

Jack whispered to Louisa, 'That's great news! The pedlar can't have set sail. He must still be here.'

Louisa turned to the wrinkled sailor. 'We're trying to find someone. A man with a rainbow-coloured coat carrying a huge rucksack. Have you seen him? He might have arrived this morning.'

'I did see a fella as fits that description. Shifty-looking chap. Trying to sell people his stuff.'

'That's him. Where can we find him?' asked Jack.

'Hanging around the Marinna Tavern.' The sailor nodded towards a tavern halfway along the harbour. A group of men stood by the open door.

'Thank you!' called Jack, heading in that direction.

'Wait,' said Louisa, catching his coat sleeve. 'What do we do when we find the pedlar? How are we going to make him give us the snowflakes?'

Jack was thoughtful. 'Let's stay out of sight. See if we can spot him first. Then we can work out a plan.'

Louisa nodded.

They kept close to the row of chalets, staying in the shadows. They could hear laughter and the clanking of tankards as they approached the tavern. They crept up to a side window and peered into the crowded room. The pedlar was easy to spot. He was leaning against the bar, a drink in his hand, his huge rucksack on his back, taking up the space of several people.

'There he is,' said Jack.

Louisa pressed her face against the cold glass. A purple-faced merchant burst through the door. 'There you are, you scoundrel! Sell me fake gems, would you?' He pushed through the crowd towards the pedlar. He grabbed his rucksack and spun him around. 'What do you call this, hey? These were shining brightly this morning, now look at 'em! Worthless filth!' The merchant shook a fistful of blackened jewels in the pedlar's face.

Louisa gasped. 'Jack! It's the snowflakes!'

'He sold them?' said Jack, puzzled. 'He can't have known they have magic powers!'

The merchant raised his fist, threatening to punch the pedlar. 'I want my money back, do you hear? No one double-crosses me and gets away with it!'

'That's enough, you two!' boomed a voice from the other side of the bar. A tall man, with a belly the size of a beer barrel, strode towards them. He caught the pedlar and the merchant by their collars, almost lifting them off the ground. 'I won't stand for that kind of behaviour in my bar. Out! The pair of you!' With that he carried them to the door and tossed them outside. Jack and Louisa dashed to the front of the tavern in time to see the men thump into the snow with the black diamond snowflakes scattering around them.

'Now!' hissed Jack. 'Grab the snowflakes!' He lunged at the diamonds.

Louisa hesitated, scared of being caught by the pedlar or the angry merchant. The pedlar shook his head groggily and tried to stand.

'Quick!' hissed Jack, snatching up a diamond snowflake.

Louisa bobbed down and scooped up the four diamonds closest to her. Nearby, the merchant stirred. The pedlar rose to his feet. Jack tugged Louisa's arm, pulling her away. 'Let's go!' he cried.

The pedlar launched himself at Louisa and caught her arm.

'Stealing from me, young lady?'

'They're not yours! You stole them from my friend!' cried Louisa.

'Wish I hadn't. They've caused me nothing but trouble.'

'Let us have them, then!' cried Jack.

The pedlar's eyes narrowed. A look of recognition crossed his face. 'I've seen you before, haven't I?'

Louisa twisted her wrist, caught in his tight grip. 'Let me go!'

He held her firmly. A flicker of greed showed in his yellowed eyes. 'If your friend wants the snowflakes so badly, perhaps they are not worthless after all. You're not taking them anywhere.'

Behind him, the merchant staggered to his feet. 'You cheat! You're not getting away with this! I want my money!'

The pedlar stepped away from him, easing his grip on Louisa. At once she squirmed out of his hold. 'Come on, Jack!' she cried and fled back along the dock, pushing past sailors and dodging fishing nets.

'Hey! What's the rush?' cried one seaman, stumbling out of her way.

Behind her, she could hear Jack panting. 'Keep going, Louisa!' he cried. 'The pedlar is chasing us!'

Louisa ran, not daring to look over her shoulder, when she heard a piercing whistle from the far end of the dock. She froze. Jack skidded and bumped into her. 'Look over there!' she cried. Ahead, lit by the yellow lamplight and standing on a crate to survey the crowd, was a tall guard in a green uniform. He was pointing in their direction, blowing his whistle repeatedly.

Sailors and merchants turned to stare at Jack and Louisa, muttering suspiciously among themselves.

'Jack! It's the guard! The one who chased us from the square. He's found us!'

The crowd outside the tavern parted as a man with a large rucksack headed their way. 'The pedlar is still chasing us too!' cried Jack.

'What can we do?' wailed Louisa. 'We're trapped!'

# Chapter 13
## Chaos

The guard and the pedlar closed in on them. Louisa felt like a rabbit caught in a snare. Her heart hammered against her ribs.

'Got yourselves in a spot of trouble?' wheezed a shrivelled old sailor nearby. 'Been up to no good?'

Jack and Louisa backed away until they were at the edge of the quay. Below them, the sea slapped against the harbour wall.

'We've done nothing wrong!' said Jack.

'Really? Maybe there's a nice reward out for

whoever catches you,' the man sneered.

Jack nudged Louisa with his elbow. He unfurled his fist enough for her to glimpse the diamond snowflakes he had taken. 'Use your snowflakes!' he whispered.

Louisa frowned. 'They're damaged. They won't work properly. They'll cause chaos!'

Jack grinned. 'Exactly!'

Louisa stared at the blackened diamond snowflakes in her hand. *Which magical power do you have?* Beside her, Jack tightened his fist and muttered, 'Snowstorm!'

At once the sky growled. The black cloud coiled and swirled. The men around the harbour gasped and turned their faces skyward. Louisa gaped as black snowflakes started to fall. They fluttered onto the crowd.

'Urgh! What is it?' the sailors cried, rubbing the coal-like flecks from their faces and coats.

Before they realised what was happening, a freezing wind blew in from the sea, striking them with a blizzard of black snow. Confused and frightened, the seamen collided with one another as they tried to find cover.

Jack nodded at Louisa. She smiled. Their plan was working. She slipped her hand inside George's pouch and held the diamond snowflakes he had given them. 'Help us not to be seen!' she said softly. She watched in awe as her feet, legs and waist vanished. She glanced at Jack. The magic had crept up to his neck and stopped. His head was left hovering on an invisible body.

'Ghosts!' wailed a nearby sailor. The colour drained from his weathered face.

'Your head isn't invisible!' Jack hissed.

'Neither is yours!' Louisa hissed back, grinning.

The sailors shrank away from them. Just then the pedlar broke through the crowd. He halted when he saw Jack and Louisa's floating heads. His jaw dropped. His eyes bulged.

'See? He didn't know about the magic!' said Jack. 'He's just a thief.'

'The green guard is still after us!' said Louisa, spying the uniformed man storming along the seafront towards them.

The pedlar heard the guard's whistle and looked in his direction. His face became rigid with terror. Trembling, he threw his rucksack on the ground and tried to escape.

'Stop him!' yelled the guard.

The seamen were too preoccupied with trying to find shelter from the storm to obey. In the crush, the pedlar was knocked to the ground just as the guard arrived on the scene. The pedlar cowered at his feet. The guard crouched by him and seized him by the collar. His bald head gleamed in the streetlight as he spoke to him in a low, urgent voice.

'What does the guard want with the pedlar?' asked Louisa.

'Dunno. I thought he was after us!'

'Me, too. Let's get out of here!'

Before they could move, the pedlar cried out, 'You're wrong! It's them!' He pointed at Jack and Louisa.

The guard rounded on them, releasing the pedlar's collar. His eyes flitted from their faces to their invisible bodies. He flinched. 'What on earth...?'

'Do something else!' cried Louisa.

'Animals,' said Jack. 'Beasts of the sea!'

The snow swirled. The wind howled. But there was no sign of any sea creature.

'Louisa, you must have the animal snowflake!'

Louisa gripped the four diamond snowflakes she had picked up and thought of the largest sea creature she knew. 'Whales, come!'

Above the roar of the wind, a haunting cry echoed from deep within the belly of the sea. Waves crashed against the stone wall. The cry grew louder. The row of tethered ships began to move. One by one, each vessel was lifted a metre or so out of the water before falling back into the sea, forming an enormous Mexican wave along the harbour.

'Something's swimming this way!' cried Jack.

Suddenly, out of the rolling waves emerged the shining grey hide of an enormous whale. Sheets of water slipped off its back as it rose out of the sea. The few men left on the harbour cried out in fear and ran in every direction. Louisa and Jack stood staring up at the majestic beast. It forced water out of its blowhole then sank beneath the waves, slapping its tail against the sea with a noise like a clap of thunder.

The ship closest to them pitched uncontrollably. Its main mast swung like a giant pendulum. 'Look out!' cried Louisa as the crow's nest split in two. She pulled Jack onto the jetty as it smashed onto the harbour where they had just been standing. The jetty swayed with the waves. Louisa and Jack struggled to stand. 'Get back to the harbour!' shouted Jack.

Louisa staggered towards the shore. A dark figure stepped onto the jetty, blocking her escape.

'Going somewhere?' mocked the tall guard in the green velvet uniform.

# Chapter 14
## Flight

'Why not stop this nonsense and come with me?' the guard called.

Black snow swirled around them. Louisa braced herself against the wind. She glanced at Jack. His body began to reappear. The magic was fading. He caught her eye and tilted his head towards the ship. Louisa responded to his signal and flung herself onto the deck. The guard chuckled.

'You think you can escape me?' He took a step closer to Jack.

Louisa saw the panic on Jack's face. Suddenly Jack thrust his arm towards the guard and cried out, 'Snowballs!' Instantly, a multitude of large black snowballs formed in the sky. They bombarded the guard like a swarm of angry bees.

'Urgh!' the guard shouted, stumbling and tripping over the remains of the fallen crow's nest.

Jack dived onto the ship. He landed awkwardly on his ankle and cried out in pain.

'Jack!' cried Louisa.

'I'm okay,' he said, grimacing.

'Quick! Help me free the anchor,' yelled Louisa, turning a wooden crank.

'What? You can't raise the anchor,' shouted Jack above the wailing wind. 'We don't know how to sail a ship!'

Louisa paused, feeling foolish. 'I thought that's what you wanted.'

'No! Just somewhere to hide!'

Louisa was about to answer when the guard leapt from the harbour and thudded onto the deck. 'You're not getting away from me this time!' he growled.

'What's your problem?' said Jack, hobbling to Louisa's side. 'My sister only looked under some silly tarpaulin. Where's the harm in that?'

'You think *that's* all it is?' The guard smirked.

'We've done nothing wrong! Leave us alone!' cried Louisa, shivering in the biting wind. The stress of being pursued for two days suddenly overwhelmed her. 'I just want to go home!' she cried, feeling tears stinging her eyes. 'I want to see George and Harry. To return to our friends.'

The guard changed his tactic, softening his manner. 'Of course you do,' he said gently. 'There's no need for all this unpleasantness.' A fake smile spread across his lips. 'All you need to do is come with me.'

He reminded Louisa of a snake slithering slowly towards its prey.

'No!' cried Jack. 'We're not coming with you. We have a job to do!'

The guard's face tensed with anger, and the hardness returned to his eyes. He prepared to move towards them when there was a sorrowful cry from beneath their feet.

'It's the whale,' said Louisa. 'He's underneath the ship!' She shoved all of the diamond snowflakes into one pocket and grabbed the crank for balance. Jack took hold of the handle alongside her. The vessel shuddered and creaked as the whale hit the boat, tipping it sideways.

'Argh!' cried the guard, sliding off the deck into the inky water.

Louisa shut her eyes, wishing she could open them and be safely back at George's little house. *If only we could fly away…*

'That's it!' she said, her eyes snapping open. 'Let us fly!' she commanded, wrapping her hand around the snowflakes in her pocket. At once the ship righted itself and began to drift upwards into the dark sky.

'The boat is flying!' yelled Jack.

'I only meant for us to fly,' wailed Louisa, 'not the whole ship! I warned you that the snowflakes might not be working properly.'

Below them, the twinkling street lamps grew smaller. The harbour shrank until it resembled a child's model with toy boats.

'Now what?' cried Jack as the boat drifted higher and higher into the black sky. 'You know I hate flying!' He shoved the snowflakes into his coat pocket and clung onto the crank with both hands. Below, cries of alarm rang out from the port, accompanied by a familiar rumble.

'That sounds like another earthquake,' said Louisa. 'Of course! We're taking the diamond snowflakes even further away from the mountain!'

'Can you steer this thing?' cried Jack, gritting his teeth. 'We could end up far out to sea.'

'I don't know how to steer it!' cried Louisa.

'Try telling the snowflakes!'

Louisa squeezed the diamond snowflakes. 'Fly to I-Sing!' she commanded.

The ship turned and headed inland, swerving left and right, skimming over the rooftops of Port Marinna.

'That's worse!' said Jack.

Louisa scowled. 'I'm trying!' She staggered across the deck and took the ship's wheel. 'I'll try to steer it up the mountain!'

The snowstorm buffeted the vessel and blew Louisa's hair in a tangled mass across her face. 'Can't you stop the storm?' she yelled. 'I can't see anything!'

Jack had turned a pale shade of green and looked as though he might be sick. 'Snowstorm, stop!' he murmured.

The wind obeyed and died away, but the black snow continued to fall. 'Not perfect, but better,' said Louisa, pushing her matted hair from her face. She strained against the wheel, trying to hold the ship steady, but the boat continued to swerve. 'This thing has a mind of its own! It's never going to fly us to I-Sing.'

Jack moaned. He really did look unwell. They had flown past the outskirts of Port Marinna, but were veering off to the left.

'We'll have to land,' said Louisa. 'Otherwise this thing will take us way off-course. Hold on

tight! I hope this works. Snowflake, land the ship – gently!'

The ship dropped suddenly. Louisa felt her stomach leap into her throat. The vessel crashed into a small cluster of trees with a loud crunch and the sound of snapping wood. It creaked and slid to a halt. Louisa clung on to the wheel, expecting the ship to keel over at any moment, but they remained still. Cautiously, she released the wheel and looked around. The ship was supported on either side by trees.

'We survived!' she cried. 'Let's get off this thing before the magic changes its mind!'

'I am never flying again!' moaned Jack. He let go of the crank and tried to stand. 'Argh! My ankle is killing me!'

'Let me see.' Louisa bent down to help remove his boot.

'No! Leave it alone. I can feel my foot swelling up. I don't think I can take off my boot.'

'Maybe it's broken? If I pull your boot off it might make the break worse.'

'I don't think it's broken, just badly sprained. Either way, how am I going to get back to I-Sing?'

Louisa saw the panic in his ashen face. She

unfolded her fingers and stared at the tarnished diamonds. Black snowflakes fell silently around them. She tipped her face to the sky. 'I hate this black snow. I hate that black cloud! It feels like the goodness has been sucked out of everything.'

For a moment they were silent. At last Jack spoke. 'Somehow, we have to return the snowflakes to Harry. If we don't, life here will only get worse.'

Louisa felt lost. They were stranded. Jack was injured. The world around them was falling apart. 'How am I going to return the snowflakes to Harry now?' she mumbled. The weight of the responsibility threatened to crush her. She wanted to shout at the mountain. She wanted to scream that she couldn't do it, that she had had enough.

Jack was staring up at her. 'You can't give

up now,' he said, pain etched across his face. 'You have to find a way.'

She sighed. How could she give up when Jack needed her help? 'I guess this means I'm in charge,' she said. 'I always hated being the little sister. Now that I'm the one looking after you, being the oldest doesn't seem so much fun.'

Jack smiled weakly. 'Trust me, being the oldest sucks!'

Louisa glanced around the deck. 'Well, let's start by getting you off the boat,' she said. 'There's a rope ladder over here.' She tossed the ladder over the side of the ship. 'Do you think you can make it down? At least your boot is supporting your ankle.'

'I'll try.' With Louisa's help, he limped to the side.

Louisa tugged the ladder to check it was secure. 'Right, then. Let's go!'

# Chapter 15
## Protector

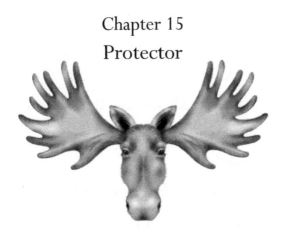

Louisa climbed to the ground then held the ladder steady for Jack. 'This is a change, me helping you to climb!'

'Ha ha,' said Jack, slipping to the ground. As he landed, one of the diamond snowflakes fell from his pocket.

Louisa bent to pick it up. A dreadful thought flashed through her mind. 'Jack, we don't know if we've got all the snowflakes! We were in such a rush to grab them outside the tavern that we didn't check that we had all ten!'

'I found three,' said Jack.

'I picked up four. That's only seven, and there are ten in total. We're missing three!'

'No, you already had the three in the pouch – the ones that George and Harry gave us. Count them.'

Louisa fished the remaining snowflakes from her pocket. 'You're right. I have seven. Phew! Thank goodness we have all ten.'

'Take mine, Louisa. You might as well have them all now that you're officially in charge.'

'Oh. All right.' Louisa felt nervous about being responsible for all the diamond snowflakes. 'Hang on. I have some string in my rucksack. I'll use it to thread them together to make a necklace, like Harry did. They'll be safer that way.'

She took out the string and threaded the diamond snowflakes on it. 'They look awful.

Black and sinister. The quicker we get them back to I-Sing, the better.'

'Don't get them muddled,' said Jack. 'Put the ones whose power we know how to use on one side. That will make them easier to use again.'

'Good idea. I'll put them in alphabetical order: create objects, help, move objects...I wonder if that's what Harry did?'

Jack gave her his diamond snowflakes.

'This one has a cobweb pattern in the middle,' said Louisa. 'Maybe it's the snowflake that communicates with animals. I'll put it first.'

Just then a soulful mooing filled the air.

Louisa stood still. 'What was that?' Quickly, she hung the string around her neck and hid the necklace inside her coat.

'We've heard that cry before, at the river and near the deserted chalet,' said Jack.

Louisa took Jack's arm. 'I wonder what it is? Come on.' Together, they edged away from the boat. After a few minutes, they emerged from the trees. A covering of fresh black snow lay before them. 'It's so creepy!' said Louisa.

'Shh! Look! Up there!' said Jack.

Standing not far away on a ridge was a regal creature with magnificent antlers.

'What is it?' murmured Louisa.

'It looks like a moose,' said Jack.

'But it's completely white! Even its antlers are covered in white fur!'

The beast grunted and tossed his head in their direction.

'He's seen us! Don't move,' whispered Jack.

'I'm not going to. I learned that lesson with the baby moose.'

The stately animal sauntered towards them. Louisa felt her legs turn to cotton wool. Beside

her, she felt Jack tremble. 'He's even bigger than Daisy,' he gasped, 'and I thought she was too big!'

The white moose halted in front of them. He lowered his head so that his eyes were on their level. He gave a low snort and extended his long nose towards them. Louisa stretched out her hand and touched his cheek. The moose rubbed his jaw gently against her glove.

'He seems friendly,' she said. 'Maybe he's the white creature that I kept seeing on our journey.'

'Could he be the animal that has been helping us?' said Jack. 'You know, perhaps he called the mother moose away when she charged at you.'

'And pushed the tree into the river to save us,' added Louisa.

The moose bobbed his head.

'Did he just nod?' asked Jack.

'No way! How is that possible? Is he magic?' said Louisa, stroking the moose's great neck.

'In the cabin you wished that we had an animal to watch over us!' said Jack. 'That was before the magic went wrong. The snowflake must have commanded the moose to look after us!'

'Doesn't the magic wear off after a short time?' asked Louisa.

'It seems to work for as long as it's needed,' said Jack.

'Do you think he'll help us get back to I-Sing?'

The moose swung his huge head towards his back then strolled to a large rock and stood beside it, like a horse waiting at a mounting block.

'I guess that's my answer. I think he wants us to ride him,' said Louisa.

'You're joking!' said Jack. 'I thought flying was bad. Riding a giant moose with no saddle is not my idea of fun.'

'With your injured ankle, you're not going to make it back to I-Sing on foot. We can't trust the diamond snowflakes to work properly to help us in any other way. This is our best hope.'

'I suppose.'

Louisa took the sleeping bags from her rucksack and laid them over the moose's back. 'That'll make it more comfy.'

'Won't they slide off? And how are we going to hold on? His fur is so short and smooth. We need a rope or something.'

'I didn't pack any rope.'

'We could use your belt.'

Louisa scowled. 'My waist is not the size of a moose!'

Jack wearied of the conversation. He flopped in the snow, holding his leg and wincing. 'I wish I hadn't twisted my stupid ankle on the boat!'

Louisa stared up at the tall ship. 'Of course! There must be rope on the boat. Why didn't I think of that sooner? Stay there while I check.' Louisa ran back to the rope ladder and climbed on board. After several minutes of searching the deck, she found a small, torn sail. Attached to one corner was a rope.

'What's that?' called Jack as she returned with the sail tucked under her arm.

'It's the best I could find.' She approached the moose and patted his neck. 'Good boy. Keep nice and still for me.' Standing on the rock, she wrapped the sail over the sleeping bags like a girth and tied the end to the rope. The moose snorted and nudged the sleeping bags with his nose. 'Sorry – I know it feels odd but you'll get used to it.'

Jack dragged himself onto the rock and, with her help, sat astride the moose. He groaned in pain as he lowered his injured leg over the moose. 'This busted ankle will ruin my chances of getting back into the rugby team!'

'You're doing really well,' Louisa encouraged him. 'Hold on to the rope.'

'I am already!' said Jack, clinging on for dear life.

Louisa sat behind him. 'Okay. Come on, boy,' she said to the moose. 'Take us to I-Sing!'

## Chapter 16
## Overtaken

The black snow had stopped falling. The moose headed up the mountain, away from the stranded ship, ambling along with long, lolloping strides. The movement jarred Jack's damaged ankle. 'Argh! Walking was less painful than this!'

Louisa remembered how her friend at school wore a sling to support her arm when she had broken it. She leant forwards and took the corner of the sleeping bag, then folded it over Jack's sore leg.

'Is that better?' she asked, sitting on the corner to keep it in place.

'A bit, thanks.'

'We need to get you back to I-Sing. They must have a doctor there.'

'I hope someone can help me before the snow globe sends us home. I don't fancy being transported back to Grandma's in the whirlwind with this ankle. It's too painful.'

'The magic will get us to I-Sing,' said Louisa with determination.

'I just hope this moose knows where he's going!' said Jack.

The moose gave a grunt and tossed his head.

'He certainly thinks he does! I'm not about to argue with him,' said Louisa. 'I wish he would walk faster, though. This is a snail's pace! It'll take us days to reach I-Sing.'

'As the snowflakes' magic isn't working, there's nothing else we can do,' said Jack.

Louisa sighed.

The moose weaved endlessly between the trees in the thickening forest. It felt as though they had been travelling for hours when at last they reached a wide path.

'I guess this is some sort of road,' said Louisa.

'Just with s-no-w tarmac,' said Jack. 'Get it? No tarmac, snow tarmac, because the snow is black like tarmac?'

Louisa pulled a face. 'A joke is really not funny when you have to explain it, Jack! This must be the main route between I-Sing and Port Marinna.' She pointed to the ground. 'Look, under the black snow, there are sledge marks. Other people have travelled this way.'

The moose began to follow the trail uphill. 'This must be the route that the pedlar and guard used to get from I-Sing to the port,' said Jack.

'Yes,' said Louisa thoughtfully. She replayed the scene at the harbour in her mind. 'Wasn't it odd how the guard went straight for the pedlar when he saw him, as though he was chasing him as well as us? Do you think the guard knew the pedlar had stolen the diamond

snowflakes from George's house? Was he trying to get them back?'

'Maybe George told him,' said Jack. 'George's note said that the guards had visited him and Harry and had been asking questions.'

'When the pedlar said "It's them!", he was telling the guard that we had stolen the snowflakes, not him,' said Louisa.

Jack sighed. 'I suppose we did steal them in a way. We took them from the pedlar.'

'We didn't steal them. They never belonged to him! They're Harry's. We're just returning the snowflakes to him. Surely the guard wouldn't arrest us for that!' said Louisa.

'Or maybe the guard is still angry with you for snooping about in the fountain.'

'I can't imagine why. It was just some building stuff.'

'It seems to be getting lighter,' said Jack.

Louisa gazed at the grey sky. 'You're right! The black cloud is paler. It is more like a slightly annoyed rain cloud than a world-destroying death cloud! Is it because we're taking the snowflakes closer to Harry and I-Sing? I wonder if the diamond snowflakes are less black too.' She was about to inspect the snowflakes when the moose stopped and threw up his head, almost tossing them off his back.

'Easy, whoa, there,' said Louisa.

The moose stood stone-still, twitching his floppy ears.

'Do you remember, Daisy did that when she heard something or sensed danger,' said Louisa.

'Wha—'

'Shh!'

Behind them they heard the faint sound of dogs barking and a man shouting.

'Someone's coming this way!' said Louisa. Instinctively she kicked the moose. He let out a snort of disgust.

'He's not a horse!' scolded Jack.

Louisa patted the moose's neck. 'Sorry, boy. But, please, get off the path!'

The moose strode into the forest. Louisa was grateful for the cover provided by the pine trees. The cries of the dogs grew closer. Between the branches she glimpsed a large team of huskies sprinting along the road. Behind them, standing on the sledge, was the bald guard.

'It's him!' Louisa whispered.

They watched until the barking faded and the sledge disappeared from view.

'Thank goodness he didn't see us,' said Jack.

'They'll reach I-Sing in no time at that speed,' Louisa murmured. She checked her watch. 'It's four o'clock already. We should follow the main road. It'll be quicker than zigzagging through the forest.'

The moose responded by meandering towards the road. They followed the path for over an hour when Louisa noticed that the grey cloud overhead had become completely white, and patches of blue sky peeked through growing gaps. 'The cloud is disappearing,' cried Louisa. 'It's as if the magic is healing!'

Jack didn't reply. He leant forwards on the moose's neck and mumbled something.

'Jack, are you all right?'

'I'm worn out. The pain in my ankle doesn't help. I just want to sleep.'

Louisa unzipped her coat to examine the diamond snowflakes hanging around her neck. 'Jack, the snowflakes are becoming clear again. It might be safe to ask the magic to help us.'

Jack didn't reply, but gave a limp thumbs-up.

'Jack, we've got to get you to a doctor!' Louisa's hands trembled as she cupped the diamond snowflake with the cobweb pattern. 'I'm going to help you, Jack. Hold on!' She spoke to the moose: 'Moose, run like the wind!'

# Chapter 17
## Healing

The moose let out a deep bellow. Louisa felt the magic blast from his body. The power coursed through her veins like an electric shock. She grabbed Jack's waist. The moose exploded into a headlong gallop like a racehorse released from the starting gate. His coat glowed a luminous white. Flashes of silver flew from his hooves. His body shone like shafts of sunlight. Despite the astonishing speed, the ride felt smooth and effortless.

'We're riding the wind!' cried Louisa, her

chest bursting with delight. Jack grunted a reply and clung on to the moose grimly. Trees flashed past at such a pace that they became a fuzzy haze. Louisa was amazed that no wind blew in her face. *We're not riding the wind — we've become the wind!* She felt invincible, unstoppable, hurtling through a rush of colours. She wanted the ride to last forever, but the moose's pace slowed. The light radiating from his fur faded. The blurred colours became shapes: trees, chalets, people.

'Jack, we're back in I-Sing!' cried Louisa. 'There's the village sign. We've done it! Soon Harry will have the diamond snowflakes again. Everything's going to be all right.'

'At last,' Jack murmured.

The moose slowed from a gallop to a trot then a walk. A young woman dropped her basket of groceries when she saw them. An elderly man chopping wood froze mid-swing when they passed him. 'Good gracious!' he exclaimed.

A group of boys throwing snowballs stopped their game and gawped at them. 'Wow! A white moose! I've never seen a white moose before!'

'I've never seen anyone ride a moose before!'

Louisa would have smiled and waved at them if she hadn't been so anxious to reach George's house. 'George will be so relieved to see us. Harry too. I can't wait to see their faces when we give them the diamond snowflakes.'

Jack grunted in pain. He bent forwards, resting his head on the moose's shoulder. 'My ankle hurts so much!'

Louisa's stomach lurched. 'George will know how to help you. He can take us to the doctor. I think we're almost at the square – I recognise this street. It's Portland Road, the one we ran down when we left the village.'

She wrapped her fingers around the first two diamond snowflakes. 'Moose, take us to George's house,' she instructed. 'We need help!'

The moose waggled his head in reply, making his enormous antlers sway. They entered the village square. It was the end of market day. Stall-holders had begun to pack away their goods. The last remaining shoppers were drifting home. The moose turned left and trotted past the Great Hall and the Velvet Lady's grand home. Her green flag fluttered from the mast on the roof.

'This isn't the right way!' cried Louisa. 'George's home is to the right! Moose, you're taking us the wrong way!' She tugged the sail. With no reins to steer him, she was powerless to change direction. 'This isn't the right way!' she shouted.

The moose ignored her and broke into a canter. Jack cried out in pain, gripping the rope and bouncing around like a yo-yo.

The moose thundered close to the stalls. His antler caught a display of coats, knocking the whole rail to the ground. 'Hey!' yelled the seller.

'Sorry!' called Louisa.

The seller shook his fist. 'Hooligans!'

When they reached the far end of the square, the moose swerved right. 'Whoa!' cried Jack.

'Crazy animal!' Louisa fumed.

'Tell it to stop!' yelled Jack.

'I'm trying. The snowflake isn't working! The moose isn't listening to me!'

The moose cantered along the far side of the square then turned left, heading out of the village. 'I can't hold on much longer!' cried Jack when the moose swerved down a path that led from the main road behind a ramshackle chalet with a balcony jutting out from the roof.

'Is this Madame Étoile's home?' said Louisa. 'Grandma said the old lady lived in a tumbledown house with a balcony.'

At the rear of the chalet a huge weeping willow tree stood in their way. Its branches hung in front of them like a waterfall of ice. 'Argh!' cried Louisa as they crashed through its leaves. Inside the dome of branches, the moose halted, almost flinging Jack and Louisa from its back.

'I'm glad you stopped,' said a croaky voice.

Louisa looked up. Madame stood a metre away, tying a net of birdseed to a branch. 'You're Madame Étoile!' she gasped, staring at the old lady, who was wrapped in a thick shawl and

wearing a long embroidered skirt. She was exactly as Grandma had described her.

'Quite so,' said Madame. She shuffled towards them and squinted up at Jack. She pursed her lips then turned to Louisa. 'Don't dawdle, girl. Dismount. It appears Jack needs assistance. Hurry!'

'You know our names?' said Louisa, astonished.

'Of course. I recognise you from when you came to I-Sing six months ago.'

Louisa slid from the moose's back. 'Jack's hurt his ankle. It's sprained, I think. Can you help us? I told the moose to take us to George's house, but it brought us to you instead.'

'You also asked the snowflakes to help,' mumbled Jack.

'Help often comes in the way we need it most, not in the way we would like it best,' said Madame.

'We need a doctor,' said Louisa.

'There you are! We have no doctor in I-Sing. Not since the last one died. The moose has taken you to the right place.'

Louisa slipped her hand inside her coat and touched the cobweb snowflake. Quietly, she asked the moose to kneel. The moose responded at once, enabling Jack to dismount.

'You have all manner of magic at your fingertips, I believe?' said Madame, her shrewd blue eyes studying Louisa.

'You know about the diamond snowflakes, don't you, Madame?' Louisa ventured, patting the moose's neck as he stood. Madame supported Jack, helping him to hop towards a nearby log. He sat down gratefully.

'Indeed.' Madame examined Jack's pale face. 'Something for the pain first. Yes?'

Jack nodded. Madame turned to the drooping branches and plucked several leaves from the tree. 'I was there when your grandma retrieved the diamond snowflakes from Kraus all those years ago,' she said. 'I imagine your grandma has told you the story, and about how the snowflakes were lost in the forest?'

'Yes, she did!' said Louisa. 'How did you know Rosie was our grandma?'

'Logic. Who else your age, looking so much like her, could arrive here from another world?' Madame handed the leaves to Jack. 'Chew on these. Three should do it.'

Jack put one leaf into this mouth and grimaced.

'Not delicious, but effective,' said Madame.

Soon Jack smiled. 'That's incredible! The pain's almost gone!'

'Louisa, I believe you have the diamond snowflakes?' said Madame.

'Yes. It's a long story,' said Louisa. 'We're returning them to Harry where they belong.'

'Ah, yes. When Harry appeared in the village performing magic, I guessed that he had somehow found the diamond snowflakes and was using them. My question is, where do they truly belong?' She held Louisa firmly in her gaze.

Instead of a simple question, Madame's words felt like a direct challenge. Louisa squirmed. Before she could answer, Madame spoke to Jack. 'Now to heal the sprain.' She collected clusters of white berries that hung on the willow tree and piled them on a piece of old bark.

'Our willow trees don't have berries,' said Louisa.

'It's lucky for Jack that our willow trees do,' replied Madame, pounding the berries into a mush with her fist.

'I don't have to eat that, do I?' said Jack.

Madame tutted. 'It's a poultice, silly boy. Hold still while I remove your boot.' Her old bones creaked as she knelt beside him. She took a pair of scissors out of her skirt pocket and snipped at Jack's boot until he could remove his foot without hurting his ankle. 'Hold still,' she said, cutting away his sock.

'Oh, Jack! No wonder your foot hurt,' said Louisa. 'It's black and blue.'

'Yes, it's quite impressive, isn't it?' Jack grinned, examining the massive bruise that ran from his toes to halfway up his calf.

Madame covered the bruised area with the crushed berries. 'Give me your scarf, Jack.' She wrapped the scarf around his ankle. 'This will keep the paste in place. It won't take long for the magic to work,' she said, supporting his foot on her lap.

'Magic?' said Louisa.

Madame rolled her eyes impatiently. 'Of course, magic! What else?'

'How…?' Jack began.

'The tree was a gift from Harry on my one hundred and twentieth birthday last month.'

'A magic tree?' said Louisa. 'One of the diamond snowflakes creates plants?'

'I suppose it must. He gave me a small sapling. It grew to full height in less than a week! He told me it had healing properties. Such a dear boy. I suppose he thought I was getting on a bit, and might need the tree's help.'

Louisa giggled on hearing Madame refer to Harry as a 'boy'. He was over sixty!

Madame unwound the scarf to check Jack's ankle. 'Much better,' she said.

'It's worked!' cried Jack. 'The bruising is gone! I can move it too.' He flexed his foot. He stood and took a few steps. 'It feels great! Thanks, Madame.'

'You'll be fit to play rugby again,' said Louisa, glad to see Jack back to his usual self. She held the snowflake with the triangular pattern. 'Give Jack a new pair of boots and socks.'

The moose threw back his head in surprise as a pair of socks and boots appeared from nowhere. Jack pulled them on. 'They're better than my old ones,' he said.

'We should go,' said Louisa. The moose knelt in the snow, ready for her to mount.

As she prepared to leave, Madame caught her hand and spoke to her earnestly. 'Your grandma risked her life battling against Kraus to restore the diamond snowflakes to their home – where they belong. Make the right choice. It's time for you to complete her task.'

Louisa stared back, trying to understand what Madame was asking her to do. '*Restore the diamond snowflakes to their home…Make the right choice…Complete her task.*' Grandma had found the diamond snowflakes in a cave deep inside the mountain. Was that truly where they belonged? Was Madame telling her to journey to the heart of the mountain and return the snowflakes to the cavern? The idea was unthinkable. They were so close to completing their mission. They had rescued the diamond snowflakes from the pedlar and were at the point of returning them to Harry. How could Madame ask her to begin a new quest after all they had been through?

'Goodbye, Madame,' said Louisa, stiffly. She mounted the moose behind Jack.

'Thank you!' called Jack, waving to Madame as they rode out from beneath the willow and into the street.

'What did Madame say to you?' asked Jack.

Louisa shook her head. 'You don't want to know. Moose, take us to George's house.'

## Chapter 18

## Ransom

As daylight faded in the village, lamps lit chalet windows, giving the street a warming glow. 'I hope George is cooking tea. I'm so hungry!' said Jack.

'Maybe Harry will use the diamond snowflake to make something delicious like sausage and mash,' said Louisa. 'I can't wait to warm up beside the fire.' She wriggled her numb toes.

The moose ambled along the street that led to George's house. They approached the familiar dwelling but there were no lights to welcome them home.

'I don't think anyone is in,' said Louisa.

'I'll check,' said Jack.

The moose stopped at the front door and sniffed the wood. Jack slid down his neck to the ground. 'Hello!' he called, banging on the door. 'George, Harry! It's us!'

There was no answer.

Jack knocked again. 'Where can they be?'

'What's that?' said Louisa. 'Something's nailed to the door. Above your head!'

Jack reached up. 'It's an envelope.' He tugged the paper free. 'I can't read it. It's too dark.'

'Lamp!' whispered Louisa. At once, an old-fashioned oil lamp appeared in her gloved hand. Its flame brightened the street.

'You could have used your torch,' said Jack.

'I know, but using magic is more fun!' said Louisa. 'What does it say on the envelope?'

'It's addressed to us.' Jack tore open the envelope and unfolded the letter for them to read.

To Louisa and Jack,
I have your friends.
To ensure their safe return, bring the diamond snowflake to the clearing at dusk.
Do not try to use the magic.
Your lives depend on it.

M

'Someone has taken Harry and George!' exclaimed Louisa, feeling her heart leap into her throat.

'And they want the diamond snowflakes in exchange for them!' said Jack. 'How dare they?'

'Stupid diamonds! When will they stop causing trouble?' cried Louisa. She felt a chasm of despair opening up before her, pulling her in.

'How does anyone know that we have them?' said Jack, rereading the letter. 'I wonder who M is? The pedlar? The guard?'

Louisa's tired brain began to ache. She rubbed her foredhead. 'Anyone from Port Marinna could have seen us picking up the snowflakes outside the tavern,' she said.

Jack looked up from the note. 'When is it dusk?'

'I don't know. When the sun sets? Now?'

'Then we need to find the clearing,' said

Jack. 'The letter says our lives, and probably Harry's and George's, depend on it.' He held out his hand so Louisa could help him mount the moose.

Louisa paused, took a deep breath then grabbed his wrist. 'Here we go again!' She heaved him onto the moose behind her and gave the command, 'Take us to the clearing!'

The moose trotted back along the street, through the square, then headed for Madame Étoile's road. As they passed her chalet, Madame's parting words rang in Louisa's ears: *Restore the diamond snowflakes to their home...Make the right choice...Complete her task.*

Louisa shook her head and tried to block out Madame's voice. How could she restore the snowflakes to the mountain now? She had no choice but to hand them over to whoever was holding George and Harry hostage.

# Chapter 19
## A Plan

As they left the village behind, the last rays of daylight vanished. Darkness closed around Louisa and Jack. Louisa gripped the lantern tightly, grateful for its light.

'I hope George and Harry are okay,' she said. 'I hate to think of them being taken from their home and forced into the night. Hurry, moose! Canter!' The moose gathered speed.

'Yes. I feel as though it's our fault,' said Jack. 'Whoa! How can I stay on this animal?'

'Relax! Work with the moose's movement or you'll bounce off!'

'Easy to say, harder to do!' he cried, bumping and sliding.

Louisa clutched the sail tied around the moose. 'Are we really going to hand the diamond snowflakes to this M?' she called over her shoulder. 'Isn't there anything else we can do?'

'Does M know we have ten diamonds?' panted Jack.

'Good point. We could give him five and keep five!' said Louisa, feeling a glimmer of hope. With one hand, she clasped the first diamond snowflake on the string. 'Moose, stop!' she commanded.

The moose obeyed. He threw back his antlers and skidded to a halt. Jack slammed into Louisa's back. 'Oi! Careful, Jack!'

'A little warning would be nice,' he said, rubbing his chest.

'Sorry. I'm still learning how to use these things. Here, take the lantern while I sort them out.' She removed five diamond snowflakes from the string around her neck and gave three to Jack.

He was about to stuff them inside his gloves, but paused. 'What magic powers do these have? In case I need to use them.'

Louisa twisted around and looked him fully in the face. 'We mustn't use the magic. The note told us. It said our lives depended on it.'

Jack shrugged. 'I know. I'd just feel safer knowing what powers we can use if we get into trouble. We've no idea who we might be meeting.'

Louisa shuddered at the thought of meeting their mysterious enemy. 'I suppose you're right.

You have the ones George and Harry gave us. The triangle one that creates objects, the one that moves objects and the one that helps when you're in danger. I'll keep two that I know how to use – the cobweb snowflake that controls animals and…which one did you use at the port to control the weather?'

'I think it had a sort of zigzag pattern. That one,' said Jack.

Louisa took the snowflake he was pointing at and hid it inside her glove.

Jack grinned. 'Now we're ready!'

Louisa spoke to the moose. 'Take us to the clearing!'

The moose let out a snort then pounded through the forest.

'What about the diamond snowflakes that we're giving to M?' said Jack, clinging on to Louisa. 'What powers do they have?'

'One must create plants, one makes things fly. The others, I don't know!'

They brushed against branches heavy with snow as they raced through the forest. 'Hurry!' Louisa urged. The moose grunted and lengthened his stride.

'The rope is coming loose!' cried Jack, seeing the knot around the moose's girth unravel.

'We can't stop! Grip with your knees!' yelled Louisa.

The sail holding the sleeping bags in place slackened. The sleeping bags began to slide from underneath them. 'We're going to fall!' yelled Jack.

The moose ploughed through the branches of two tall firs, showering Jack and Louisa with black snow, then came to a halt in a broad clearing where he stood, his muscles trembling, his sides heaving.

Louisa clung to his neck, gasping for breath.

'You've come at last,' said a calm, melodious voice.

In the centre of the clearing, warming herself beside a fire, was the Velvet Lady!

# Chapter 20
# A Land Far Away

'You?' cried Jack, sliding off the moose's back. A cold breeze whistled around the clearing, tugging at the lady's green robe.

'The V-Velvet Lady!' stammered Louisa. She stared at the regal woman before her. *How can she be our enemy?* she thought. 'You're...M?'

The Velvet Lady cleared her throat. 'Mayoress,' she corrected.

'Where are Harry and George?' Jack demanded.

'Have you really taken them?' said Louisa.

'I don't understand. I thought you were kind!'

'I knew she was no good,' gloated Jack.

'Show-off!'

'Come – warm yourselves by the fire,' said the Velvet Lady.

'We don't want to warm ourselves by your fire,' cried Jack. 'We want to see our friends!'

Louisa dismounted. The loose sail and sleeping bags fell into the snow. Louisa ignored them and stood at Jack's side.

'Naturally,' said the Velvet Lady. 'All in good time. I understand you have overcome many trials to retrieve the diamond snowflakes for Harry.'

'How do you know whether we have them or not?' said Jack, colour rising in his cheeks.

The Velvet Lady smiled in a superior way. 'This would all have been much easier if the pedlar had done his job properly instead of giving in to greed.'

'His job?' Louisa questioned.

'His job was to observe Harry, to discover where he kept the diamond snowflakes, then bring them to me.'

'*Bring them to you?* You mean steal them for you. That's theft!' cried Jack.

The Velvet Lady lifted her chin as if she had smelt something rather nasty. 'Theft is such a vulgar word.'

'You hired the pedlar to do your dirty work,' said Jack.

'Clearly, as Mayoress I couldn't be seen by the villagers to have anything to do with the…disappearance of Harry's belongings. The pedlar was supposed to hide the diamond snowflakes beneath the tarpaulin where the new statue is being built, ready for my guard to collect. Instead the guard found you searching there. The pedlar had fled. It is only logical that either you or the pedlar had the diamonds.'

'No wonder the guards were so determined to catch us!' Jack said quietly to Louisa.

She nodded.

The Velvet Lady stared pointedly at Jack. 'In Port Marinna, my guard discovered that you had stolen the diamonds from the pedlar. You shouldn't be so quick to accuse others of theft, my young friend.'

'We were just returning them to their rightful owner,' Jack retorted. 'They belong to Harry!'

'Do they? That's where you're wrong. You have no idea who I am, do you?'

'What do you mean?' asked Louisa.

'I come from a people who live in a land far away in the north – a harsh place. Our survival depends on our skill at hunting and our ability to build homes of ice.'

'Ice homes? You mean, igloos? You're an Eskimo?' said Louisa.

'Eskimo? Perhaps that is your name for us. Before I was born, my grandfather found a strange man wandering the ice plains, half-frozen and mumbling like a madman. Grandfather took him in and cared for him.

The man's health was poor. He lived with our family for many years until he died. During that time, Grandfather taught him our ways.

'When I was a child, this man told me stories about a village called I-Sing, a mountain, and eleven diamond snowflakes that had magical powers. These snowflakes had once belonged to him. He told me how they were lost in a clearing like this.' She gestured to the circle of trees in which they now stood. She continued, 'The man said his name was Kraus.'

'Kraus!' gasped Louisa. 'That's the teacher who took the diamond snowflakes from the mountain, Jack! When Grandma rescued her father, she used one diamond to send Kraus to a "land far away". The magic must have sent him to the north. To the Eskimos!'

'My family thought his stories were nonsense. They said he was crazy,' said the Velvet

Lady. 'They thought I was silly to believe him.' She lowered her gaze. 'I was the youngest. They never paid attention to me. They ignored me. Belittled me.'

Louisa knew how that felt. She shot Jack a sideways glance.

The Velvet Lady took a deep breath. 'I dreamt of proving them wrong – of finding the diamond snowflakes and reclaiming them in honour of Kraus. As soon as I was old enough, I travelled to this mountain in search of I-Sing and the diamonds. I lived here and searched for the diamonds for several years. Eventually, I gave up hope of ever finding them. Six months ago I became Mayoress. It wasn't the goal that I had been seeking. However, I gained a position in the village where people respected and listened to me. In a way, I had fulfilled my dream. However, soon afterwards, it all went wrong. Harry came to I-Sing. Then the earthquakes began.'

'How did you find out that Harry had the diamond snowflakes?' asked Louisa.

The Velvet Lady's gaze hardened. 'Harry is not as clever as he thinks he is. How ridiculous – hiding the snowflakes beneath his cloak on a chain around his neck! I saw them once. I'm surprised that half the village didn't see him using them every time he performed magic.'

'He was using them for good. You have no right to take the diamond snowflakes. Why should you have them?' said Louisa indignantly.

'Kraus was their original owner. Not Harry. Besides, Harry has stolen from me!' Her voice was low but laced with anger, and her cheeks blossomed pink. 'I worked my way up to this position, serving the old Mayor as his secretary. He was foolish and lazy, completely hopeless. I practically ran the village for him until he retired.

'Just when I was rewarded for my effort and was given the position of Mayoress, Harry came along with his magic tricks. He stole the admiration and respect that the villagers should have had for me! I will not be upstaged and outdone by him any more! It's time to hand the diamond snowflakes over to me. Now I will be the one who the villagers admire, not Harry! Guards! Bring them here!'

The forest echoed with the sound of several dogs barking. On the far side of the clearing, Jack and Louisa could just make out a team of husky dogs and a sledge. The two guards emerged from the shadows, leading George and Harry.

'You tied them!' said Louisa, hot with rage seeing their wrists bound with rope.

'Your friends may be elderly, but they were surprisingly slippery to arrest. Especially with that troublesome snow leopard to contend with,' said the Velvet Lady.

'What have you done with Ice-Claw?' cried Louisa.

'He's having a nice nap. He'll wake up sometime tomorrow when George returns.'

'You drugged him?' said Louisa, aghast.

'A few sleeping pills. Quite harmless.'

The guards approached the fire. Louisa saw Harry's shoulders droop wearily. He stumbled in the snow.

'George! Harry! Are you all right?' she cried, preparing to run to them.

The guards raised their staffs. Jack blocked her with his arm and shook his head. 'Not yet,' he whispered. 'Not yet.'

# Chapter 21
## Pretence

'It's fine,' called George. 'This is all some silly misunderstanding.'

Light from the bonfire flickered on their faces. Harry turned to the Mayoress, who was standing on the opposite side of the fire. 'Really, Mayoress, do you want the villagers to hear how you've treated us?'

'You have been treated perfectly well. You've been given a comfortable sledge ride here with warm blankets and a hot drink,' she replied. She turned to Louisa and Jack. 'What

I want is those diamonds! Now, hand them over. Then you can return to I-Sing with your friends.'

Louisa searched Harry's face for an answer.

'It's all right. Do what you must,' he said.

Louisa sighed deeply. She took the string of diamond snowflakes from around her neck and trudged through the snow. 'They're yours,' she said, holding out the necklace for the Velvet Lady.

The diamond snowflakes twirled in the breeze, twinkling. A look of wonder illuminated the Velvet Lady's face. She took the string and held it aloft to admire the glittering jewels. Then her face fell. She glared coldly at Louisa. 'Is this some kind of joke? There are only five diamond snowflakes here.'

Her intense stare bored into Louisa, examining her for the truth. Louisa's pulse quickened. She felt transparent, as if the Velvet Lady could see her every secret.

'That's all we have,' Jack lied. 'You've got what you want. Now let George and Harry go!'

'Not quite. Guard, search them.'

Gustav, the plump guard with the walrus moustache, strode in their direction. Louisa turned to Jack. She saw his jaw clench. He raised a fist and cried out, 'Flames, move!' At his command, flames leapt from the bonfire. They spiralled into a giant ball and hovered in the air. The moose bellowed. He trotted to the edge of the clearing, keeping a watchful eye on the fire. Jack controlled the flames and swung his hands towards the oncoming guard. The fire moved with his action, blocking the guard with a blazing wall.

'Well done!' cried Harry from somewhere beyond the fire.

Gustav tried to dodge around the inferno. Jack moved the flaming wall sideways to prevent him from passing.

Just then the second guard, having crept unseen behind the bonfire, appeared behind the Velvet Lady. He thundered towards Louisa. Her mind whirled. She held up both hands. *Left or right? Animals or weather?* The guard was almost upon her. She shut her eyes. 'Hailstorm, chase him!' she cried.

She heard the guard cry out in astonishment. She opened her eyes to see him being bombarded by large hailstones that were falling from his own private rain cloud.

'Urgh!' he yelled, batting away the balls of ice. The downpour was so relentless that, at last, he gave up and ran for cover in the forest, pursued by the cloud.

Louisa giggled. 'That'll teach him!'

Jack thrust his arm upwards, sending the fire wall shooting into the night sky where the flames evaporated. Pointing at the guard, he cried out, 'Chains!' Heavy metal chains appeared on the guard's ankles and wrists. He tried to move, but was held fast, and toppled into the snow.

'Bravo!' cried George, shaking his tied hands in salute.

'Penknife!' said Jack. Louisa saw something drop into the snow at his feet. He bent to pick it up, then hurried past Gustav, who was still writhing in the snow, to reach George and Harry.

*Good. He's going to cut their ropes!* thought Louisa.

'I warned you not to use the magic!' said the Velvet Lady sternly. Holding the five snowflakes, she stepped closer to Louisa.

'Moose, help!' Louisa cried. Immediately she heard the familiar thud of the moose's hooves. He pounded towards her from the edge of the clearing. He cut in front of the Velvet Lady and halted. His ears flattened. He lowered his head and began smacking his lips.

Instead of being afraid, the Velvet Lady dropped eye contact with the beast and calmly reached out to touch his muzzle. The moose let

out a long sigh, waggled his antlers and relaxed. Louisa stared in surprise. 'No way!'

The Velvet Lady levelled her gaze at her. 'People have underestimated me all my life.'

Louisa felt her courage dissolve. She stumbled backwards. *Now what?* Across the clearing she saw Harry and George with their hands freed. They were walking away from Jack, heading towards the husky sledge. The Velvet Lady drew closer. Her perfume reached Louisa, wafting over her like a garden of roses.

'Jack, help!' she yelled.

From across the clearing, Jack cried, 'Move!' He raised his arm. As he did, the Velvet Lady was lifted into the air. Although she was suspended above the ground, she remained poised and unflustered.

Jack ran to Louisa's side.

'Foolish children!' said the Velvet Lady. 'You

forget that I have five magic snowflakes myself!'
She held up the necklace in her right fist.

'But we know how to use our diamond
snowflakes. You don't know what yours do!'
cried Jack.

The Velvet Lady slid back her cream fur
hood and placed the string of diamond
snowflakes around her neck. 'Perhaps not. But
I know what this diamond does.' She
unbuttoned a pocket on her cloak and took out
another diamond snowflake.

'Look at that! Jack, it's twice the size of our
diamond snowflakes!' whispered Louisa.

'You're right. It's massive.'

The gem sparkled in the Velvet Lady's hand
as she held it up for them to see. 'This is the
eleventh and final diamond snowflake.'

'Oh no!' breathed Louisa. 'It's the one from
the fountain, Jack! She found it after all. It's the

snowflake that transports people to other places. Without it, we can't get back home!'

'I can see by your faces that you know the power of this snowflake,' said the Velvet Lady, smiling. 'I warned you that your lives depended on exchanging the snowflakes without using magic against me.'

'Do you know what it does?' called Jack. He shrugged at Louisa. 'She might not know. She might be bluffing.'

'When you left I-Sing six months ago, I was working late in the Mayor's office overlooking the square. I saw the fountain light up and send you home. Kraus told me that only one snowflake lights up when it performs magic — the one that transports people to other places. Why do you think I had the fountain dug up? Now I have it.'

'She does know,' said Jack. 'That's it. She's

won. We have to give her all the diamonds. It's our only hope of returning home.' He lowered his arm. The Velvet Lady floated gracefully to the ground.

Louisa's heart dropped like a stone. 'We've failed. After everything we've been through, we've failed Harry and Madame Étoile,' she murmured.

The Velvet Lady held out her left palm. 'This time I'll have all the diamond snowflakes, please. Then you may use this snowflake to return home.' In her right hand, she twirled the final diamond between her thumb and forefinger.

Jack began to remove the snowflakes hidden in his gloves.

The Velvet Lady beamed. 'That's better. At last the diamond snowflakes will be with me, where they belong.'

*Belong.* The word sent a jolt through Louisa like a bolt of lightning. Madame Étoile's words flooded her mind – *where they belong*. She knew at once what she must do.

'No!' she cried. She launched herself at the Velvet Lady. As she did, shafts of light radiated from the diamond snowflake in the Mayoress's hand. Louisa grabbed the diamond, clasping the Velvet Lady's hand along with it. 'Take us to the heart of the mountain!' she yelled.

'Louisa!' cried Jack, seizing her arm. A gust of wind coiled around them and scooped them up into a tornado of snow.

The clearing disappeared beneath them as they were lifted high into the sky. Louisa felt herself being squeezed like an orange. Jack and the Velvet Lady were shrinking beside her. She shut her eyes and hoped it would soon be over.

# Chapter 22
## Where They Belong

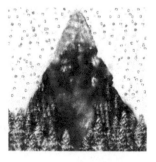

They plunged into warm, deep water. Panic clutched at Louisa's chest. Her heavy clothes dragged her down. She wriggled out of the straps of her rucksack, letting it sink out of sight. She kicked for the surface, desperate for air, and emerged gasping for breath. On either side of her, Jack and the Velvet Lady bobbed in the water.

'Over here!' spluttered Jack, doggy-paddling in the direction of a grey marble shore.

Louisa and the Velvet Lady followed. With

the weight of her clothes, Louisa found swimming exhausting. Although the edge was only a few metres away, she felt as though she had swum the length of a swimming pool. Just when she felt that all her strength had gone, her fingertips touched the edge. Gratefully, she hauled herself onto the marble and staggered to her feet.

Standing on dry land, bedraggled and dripping wet, was the Velvet Lady. She glared at Louisa. 'Where have you brought us, stupid girl?'

'She's not stupid!' said Jack, shaking the water from his ears. 'She's brave and clever!'

Louisa blinked, taken aback by Jack's words. 'It's the heart of the mountain,' she said, looking up at the perfectly round cavern, lit by two huge glass balls of fire. A third glass ball was empty. In front of them, giant stalagmites and stalactites joined to form an immense barrier.

Across the lagoon, on the far wall, streaks of white formed a star pattern.

'The shooting star!' she breathed. 'This is where Kraus and Grandma found the diamond snowflakes. *This* is where they belong.'

'What rubbish!' spat the Velvet Lady. 'Why should I leave them here on some grubby wall? Why shouldn't they belong to me? Think of all the good I could do with them to help the people of I-Sing.'

'Your world only exists because of the magic of these diamond snowflakes,' said Jack. 'They hold your world together! When they were taken from the mountain, the magic went wrong. That's why I-Sing had earthquakes. I took a snowflake out of the snow globe when we left. The magic caused chaos in my world – and yours. That's why we came back – to return the snowflakes.'

'When the pedlar took the diamond snowflakes to Port Marinna, away from the mountain, the magic went wrong again,' Louisa added.

The Velvet Lady studied them both carefully. 'So I'll keep them in I-Sing and use the magic as Harry did. Then they won't cause any harm.'

'Don't you see?' said Louisa. 'The diamond

snowflakes have caused nothing but harm since Kraus took them from this cavern! They've made people become greedy, made them steal and tell lies.'

'They've made people jealous too,' said Jack.

The Velvet Lady flinched.

'They tore apart two brothers, Harry and George, and almost destroyed your world,' said Louisa.

The Velvet Lady bit her lip and frowned. 'You don't understand. I want – I *need* the diamond snowflakes. How else will the people of I-Sing respect me? Like me?'

'They do like you,' said Louisa. 'I liked you before you arrested my friends.'

'Harry says you're clever and good at your job too,' said Jack.

'Really?' said the Velvet Lady, her face dawning with hope.

'You don't need the snowflakes for people to respect you,' said Louisa. She took the diamond snowflakes from her gloves and offered them to the Velvet Lady. 'The greatest thing you can do for I-Sing is return the snowflakes to their proper place.'

'What about your friend, Harry?' asked the Velvet Lady. 'You were going to give the snowflakes to him.'

'He's enjoyed helping others with the magic, but I think he's ready for a rest,' said Louisa.

The Velvet Lady squared her shoulders and lifted her chin. 'Right. Let's do it!'

# Chapter 23
## Shooting Star

'How do we return the diamond snowflakes to the wall?' asked the Velvet Lady.

'Why don't we lay them all out and arrange them first?' Louisa suggested.

'Good idea,' said Jack.

'Use this.' The Velvet Lady removed her soggy green cloak and laid it on the marble floor. 'It doesn't seem right to place something so precious straight on the ground.'

Jack and Louisa agreed. The Velvet Lady placed the largest diamond snowflake – with the power to transport people to other places – in the centre. 'We should arrange the others around it,' she said.

Once they had positioned the eleven diamond snowflakes, they stood back and admired their work. 'Oh,' said Jack, suddenly, 'there's one thing we haven't thought of, Louisa. If we return the snowflakes to the wall, how do we get home?'

'He's right. How will any of us get out of this cavern?' asked the Velvet Lady.

'I don't know!' said Louisa. 'All I know is that we have to return the snowflakes to their rightful place. Beyond that, we can only trust the magic.'

Jack huffed. 'Not the best plan!'

Louisa spied the hole in the stalagmites that Grandma had created to escape the cavern years earlier. 'Over there! Beyond that gap there's a tunnel, which leads out of the mountain to the glacier,' she said. 'At least we can make it back to I-Sing.'

The Velvet Lady stared at the hole, then at Louisa. 'If you are unable to return to your world, I will ensure that you are given a home in I-Sing.'

Jack grunted.

'What he means is, thank you,' said Louisa. 'That's very kind.'

'It's the least I can do.'

'Jack, you had the diamond snowflake with the teardrop pattern that moves objects. Why don't you command it to send the diamonds back to the wall?' suggested Louisa.

Jack peered down at the snowflakes. 'It's this one,' he said. He gave it to Louisa. 'You give the command. This is your idea. You were the one who was brave enough to bring us here.'

Louisa took the jewel. Light danced on its surface, making it shimmer and glitter. 'Goodbye,' she whispered. She laid the diamond snowflake on her open palm and extended her arm. 'Send all eleven diamond snowflakes back to their place on the cavern wall, never to be removed again!'

At once the ground shuddered. The snowflake flew from Louisa's hand and hovered above her. The ten diamond snowflakes lying on the cloak shot into the air and joined together, forming a dazzling star. The diamond snowflake in the centre shone a brilliant white, sending beams of light across the cavern.

'It's the shooting star!' cried Jack, shielding his eyes.

The diamond formation soared over the lagoon then struck the wall with force, embedding itself in the marble. The cavern

trembled. The mountain roared. Fresh streaks of white tore through the marble. The central diamond exploded with light, shining as brightly as the sun.

'That's done it!' cried Jack. 'Let's get out of here!'

Louisa whirled around. 'Head for the gap in the stalagmites,' she cried. 'We must get to the tunnel!' Before she could move, the stalagmites groaned and began to shake. The archway collapsed. Rocks tumbled in its place, blocking their escape. 'Now what?' she yelled. 'That was our only way out!'

Jack opened his mouth to answer when a strong wind blew around the cavern. It skimmed across the lagoon, churning it into a whirlpool. As the power of the wind increased, it lifted them clear off the ground.

'Not this again!' cried the Velvet Lady.

'I'd like to say you get used to it,' yelled Louisa, spinning above the lagoon, 'but I'd be lying!' Her body felt squeezed, as if she had pulled on clothes two sizes too small. Then suddenly they were falling.

'I hate this bit!' yelled Jack.

They smacked into a deep drift of snow in a tangled heap. Louisa's head spun so much that at first she couldn't tell which limbs were hers.

'Oi, your foot is in my face!' said Jack.

'Sorry,' said Louisa. She sat up, feeling the warmth of the bonfire on her cheeks. 'We're back in the clearing!'

Overhead, stars twinkled in the night sky. Nearby, someone chuckled. 'I would have thought that you'd land with more elegance after the amount of practice you two have had!' It was George. He smiled down at them, a mischievous glint in his eye.

'George!' cried Louisa, leaping up and giving him a hug. 'I'm so glad you're safe.'

'You're sopping wet!' he said, pulling away.

'And freezing cold!' said Jack, through chattering teeth.

George fetched their sleeping bags and a

blanket from the husky dog sledge that stood a few metres away. 'I picked up these. Yours, I believe?' He handed the sleeping bags to Jack and Louisa.

'Let me help you, Madame Mayoress,' said Harry, offering his hand to a rather dishevelled Velvet Lady, still sprawled in the snow.

Louisa pulled the sleeping bag tightly around her shoulders. She turned to Harry. 'I'm sorry we don't have the diamond snowflakes to give you. We returned them to the heart of the mountain. No one can have them now.'

'So that's where you've been.' He sighed. 'To tell the truth, that's a relief. The responsibility of protecting them has worn me out with worry these past months. Besides, I'm exhausted, constantly called upon to use their magic for others. I'm looking forward to a change. No doubt I shall miss having them, though. Using their magic has made life easier.'

'Yes, you'll have to learn how to cook! It's about time,' said George, giving his brother a friendly nudge in the ribs. 'And you'll have to learn how to iron your own cloaks!'

Harry wagged his finger at George. 'That's where you're wrong. That's what little brothers are for!'

Everyone laughed.

'I owe you both an enormous apology, Harry,' said the Velvet Lady. 'I should never have tried to take – er, steal – the diamond snowflakes from you. I'm not fit to be Mayoress. I plan to resign in the morning.'

'You'll do no such thing!' said George, handing her the blanket.

The Velvet Lady's eyes widened. 'Surely you can see it is impossible for me to go on being Mayoress after this?'

Harry took her hand. 'You're the best leader this village has ever had. It would be a crime for you not to continue being our Mayoress.'

The Velvet Lady swelled with pride. 'Then I shall do the best job I can. Perhaps somehow I can make it up to you?'

'I know,' said Louisa. 'You can forget building the statue in the village square and rebuild the fountain.'

'Good idea,' said George.

Across the clearing the white moose tossed his head and bellowed.

'I think he agrees, too,' said Louisa.

They watched him turn and lollop into the forest. A dull ache settled on Louisa's chest. 'I suppose we'll never see him again.'

'Ah, but at least you *have* seen him. A white moose! Such a rare sight – you are one of the lucky few,' said George. 'Now we must head back to the village and get you warm and dry. Fortunately we have your husky sledge, Mayoress.'

The Velvet Lady scanned the clearing. 'What about my guards, Gustav and Horace?'

'When you left, Gustav's chains disappeared. Once he was free, he didn't hang about. Bolted for the village. Haven't seen Horace. Hopefully his rain cloud has disappeared too!' George grinned.

The snow crunched beneath their boots as they headed for the sledge. 'I guess we're trapped in the snow globe now,' said Jack softly.

'I know. I wish we could go back to Grandma's,' said Louisa. 'She'll be missing us.'

Just then, a loud bang echoed through the forest. 'What was that?' cried Jack, staring at the sky. A powerful light flashed overhead and he and Louisa were lifted into the air.

George and Harry gazed up at them.

'We're going home!' Louisa called. 'Goodbye, George and Harry! Goodbye, Mayoress!'

Louisa clutched the sleeping bag as they started to spin, and the clearing vanished.

# Chapter 24
## Another Adventure?

'We did it!' cried Louisa, sitting in a heap of black and white snow in the centre of Grandma's lounge. 'I thought we were going to be trapped inside the snow globe forever. What a relief to see Grandma's things! Hello sofa, bookcase, and fireplace. Oh Jack, it's good to be back!'

'I hope there's something to eat. I'm so hungry I could eat a moose!'

Louisa glared at him.

He held up his hands in protest. 'Only kidding!'

'Ha ha!' Louisa scowled. She stood and shook the snow off her sleeping bag. 'I'm glad I didn't leave this in the snow globe. I lost my rucksack, though. It sank in the lagoon.'

'Mine too,' said Jack, clambering out of the snow pile. 'I would have drowned if I'd kept it on.'

Poking out of the snow by Jack's foot was the snow globe. Louisa picked it up. For a moment, she gazed at the snow drifting around the tiny chalets. 'I suppose we'd better put this back before Grandma sees us with it.'

'I think when she sees her lounge knee deep in snow, she'll realise that we've had it out of the cabinet!' said Jack.

'Oh…right. We ought to help clear up. I guess now that you have returned George's snowflake to the snow globe, your life will return to normal, Jack. No more pirouettes and random singing!'

Jack frowned. 'Definitely not! I hope I can become rugby captain again. I can't believe I was stupid enough to steal the snowflake from George in the first place. I've caused so much trouble.'

'The snowflakes made lots of people behave foolishly,' said Louisa, crossing the room. 'At least you returned George's snowflake and put things right.'

'Do you think we'll ever go inside the snow globe again?' asked Jack.

Louisa shrugged. 'Who knows?'

'I think I'd like a different kind of adventure next time,' Jack mused, brushing the snow from his jeans. 'Perhaps somewhere warm.' His eyes lit up. 'Hang on, wasn't Great-Grandad a craftsman? Grandma said he made the snow globe. I wonder if he made anything else that has magic powers…'

'Jack, don't get any wild ideas,' Louisa cautioned. She gently placed the snow globe on the cabinet shelf. 'I've had far too much adventure for my liking.'

'A little more adventure wouldn't hurt,' said Jack.

Louisa stood back and admired the snow globe. 'Not for me. I'm just happy to be back at Grandma's house.' She closed the glass doors and watched the final snowflakes settle on the miniature rooftops. As they did, a feeling of contentment washed over her. At last, their friends inside the snow globe were safe and well.

# Enjoyed
## *Menacing Magic?*

Then you'll love the
first two books in the

## *Secrets of the Snow Globe*
series!